THE GREAT FOG

THE GREAT FOG

And Other Weird Tales By

H. F. HEARD

AUTHOR OF "A TASTE FOR HONEY," ETC.

WILDSIDE PRESS

The short story "The Great Fog," was originally published in HARPER'S MAGAZINE, *copyright, 1943, by H. F. Heard.*

The other stories in this book have not hitherto been published.

To Christopher Wood,

These Samples and Simples

C O N T E N T S

THE GREAT FOG

THE CRAYFISH

"VERTIGO. WELL, THAT'S all there's to it. Vertigo—a pretty word." Sergeant Skillin was a psychologist and an Irishman. He believed in word-association tests, even with himself. He loved words for themselves and, so, he'd remark, they'd often give him insights all by themselves. "Oh, prettiness be damned," was, however, the association reflex he awoke in his companion. Dr. Wendover was a logician and looked it. "The truth is always there, staring you in the face," he'd say. "Every diagnostician knows that, if only he could see it." He added now, "Truth's grim face is looking at us now, but I must say it's baffling, damned baffling."

Sergeant Skillin had called in Dr. Wendover for "a second opinion," because he agreed with the opinion just expressed. The two men had different methods, but they agreed, generally, in co-operating on a difficult case and they agreed that this was a particularly difficult one. This time their agreement started from scratch—neither of them believed the verdict. But to disbelieve a verdict and to upset it—here again they were in complete accord—are two different and far-apart things.

"Now, stop your free-word-association mantras. They're nothing but mental flatulence. Tell the story over again, right from the beginning."

Sergeant Skillin was lifelong trained to bear with the tantrums of authorities. He sat down in the big desolate room, in which half-withered hangings drooped from the walls, and took out his big, well-kept notebook. Dr. Wendover strode up and down the bare floor while he was read to:

"It was common knowledge that Howard Smirke didn't get on with his wife. She was friends with Gray Gilmore but wouldn't have a divorce. Most people thought that she and Gray were simply friends. And Smirke himself didn't really want the divorce, since she had the money. He had been making a good deal as a popular doctor but had probably been spending more.

"That's the commonplace story up to last week. Then it took this turn toward strangeness. For no one expected her to be so obliging as to die quickly and cleanly—no long illness and hospital charges. She just fell dead. Heart, of course, was the popular verdict, for Dr. Smirke was the popular one of the two. But the inquest didn't bear out the *vox populi*. The autopsy had shown a perfectly sound organ, surrounded by perfectly sound organs. She should have lived for years. She was a typically healthy woman of thirty-five. Yet the other possible verdict, Foul Play, has also failed to get an innings. She died suddenly, but not secretly. To be exact, six people saw her die. And the autopsy which found her heart and other organs without a trace of disease found them also without trace of poison or toxin. True, her husband was in the same room with her when she died"—Sergeant Skillin waved his book to indicate that this was the place—"but he was not near her. Again the evidence was sixfold. The six witnesses were all between the husband and the wife at the moment of death. A couple reached her before he did. They averred that when they picked her up her neck was broken. There must have been heart failure, and then she crashed, breaking her neck.

"The six—three married couples—had been asked to dinner at the Smirke home. It was two days before Christmas. At dinner Marion Smirke had said, Would they like to help them after dinner to decorate the big studio out in the garden?" Again the Sergeant waved his book to outline the stage.

"They were having a big party there on Christmas Eve. The diners, when they entered, found coiled-up garlands of greenery on the floor here and spent some time draping them on the window frames and looping them along the walls. Finally only one great swag remained to go up. It was to hang the whole length of this long room. Depending from this great boa of foliage was the motto, 'A Happy Welcome to a Happy Home.' 'You must let Marion and me hoist this signal,' said Smirke. 'You can all help us get it into line, but we'll make it fast.' "

"So the six stood along the length of the room, holding the long, wreathed bundle of leaves up in their arms, while Howard Smirke at one end and Marion at the other mounted the tall trestle ladders, which stood at either end and reached some fifteen feet off the floor. (There they stand now, as they stood that night.) Mr. Binton, who was nearest Smirke, was given a bamboo pole with a small 'u' at the top of it. He was told to fit this into a loop which ended the cord holding the whole long garland together. When he raised it as high as he could, Smirke, bending down so that his head was level with the top step of his ladder, could just take the cord. At the other end of the line (up here), Mrs. Gortch was following out the same instructions. She had been chosen because she was tall. And Marion Smirke, bending down, also reached for the upstretched cord—reached cautiously out till her head, also, was level with her ladder's top step.

"Mrs. Gortch and the two at her end of the line stated that they were actually watching Marion to see if she had got hold of the cord, and to help her as much as they could in raising the long garland, though it wasn't heavy. She stretched her left hand down a little further. Her right was firmly on the top of the ladder. The ladder was perfectly firm. (Try it: you'll find that it is.) Marion's head came a little lower. She was quite at her ease, and cool. She had said, before climbing up, that she wasn't the least inclined to be giddy and that she actually liked heights. And, from the top of the ladder as she bent over and down, she remarked, 'I can stretch quite safely a little further, if I curl over a little more like a wilting flower.' Her head was now level with the top platform step of this ladder. Her right ear must have actually been touching it. Both her feet were on lower steps. She was perfectly supported. They all say that. Looking up at her, they saw her just keel over. Mrs. Gortch, who was nearest and was just missed by the falling body, thought she heard her gasp something, just as she let go, like 'Gray.' But that was dismissed as accretional evidence. Perhaps she had made a sound, a cry of some sort, as she slipped. She never made any after she fell. She fell right on her head on this hardwood floor—just there. Shocking, but for her as quick an end as you could imagine. Mrs. Gortch kind of fainted. I suppose it is a bit vertiginous to see that you've missed death by a hairbreadth and through your hostess literally throwing herself at your head and killing herself at your feet."

"Reflections blur impressions. Go on with the evidence," ordered Wendover.

"Two other guests, however, raised Marion—a Mr. and Mrs. Lenton. They saw that she was dead. Mr. Binton, up at the other end there, says he didn't know what had happened. Thinks he heard a crash, but knows the first thing he was sure of was that Smirke, at whom he'd been looking up, took a flying leap, almost over *his* head, to the ground, and rushed up the room. There was a group already around Marion then. Smirke pushed them aside, knelt down, took her hand, called to her, seemed beside himself."

"Um, actor-proof part, as our theatrical friends put it," Dr. Wendover couldn't resist commenting.

Sergeant Skillin patiently resumed: "After a few moments of dumb grief—that was the majority's opinion, though Mr. Binton said that he groaned—he arose quickly, saying (correctly), 'We must call the police.' Everyone acted correctly; I took the call myself; came right over here at once. They hadn't even moved the body. Told them they'd acted rightly, though against their natural but wrong feelings."

" 'What the soldier said,' or the sergeant, 'is not evidence,' " sententiously quoted Dr. Wendover.

"But it can be germane," Skillin countered quietly, and began to mutter to himself, "Germane, German, Germ."

"Stop that and go on with this," ordered the Doctor, stopping beside the seated sergeant and pointing magisterially to the open notebook.

"There isn't much more. I began by going over the autopsy

and verdict. She's away in the mortuary (we're lucky she's not under ground), and Smirke's away, 'recovering from the shock.' Case is closed and closed pretty tight. And here we are, sitting on the site and wondering how to sight a crack that will let us prize it open again."

He stared at the hard smooth floor onto which the woman had death-dived, as though some dent might be visible in it and give a clue.

"Who's in the house now?" Dr. Wendover roused him.

"Of course, the maid who let us in."

"Well, she comes next. Call her in, will you."

Mary Holster was a good witness; Dr. Wendover, was a good examiner. His manner changed as soon as she came in. He knew how to make a witness easy and open. He hardly looked at the questionee but spoke as though they were bent on a puzzle together. "Having made an incision," he used to remark to Skillin, "the task is to prevent the mental flow clotting. Nearly everyone wants to talk and can remember if they are not frightened."

"I feel sure it was quite an accident," Mary volunteered at once.

"Why?"

"Because, though I wasn't present at the actual accident, I saw exactly why it happened."

"How?"

"It was the very afternoon before the dinner party. The garlands were all here, coiled up on the floor, as they'd been delivered. And at lunch. . . ."

"Did they have any wine at lunch?" interjected the sergeant.

"No," and she ran on, "Doctor said, 'Let's see if we can get the studio decorated this afternoon.' I remember it so well, because he turned to me—I was by the sideboard—and said, 'Mary, will you give us a hand after lunch?' As soon as I'd finished clearing up, I came down here. They'd not put up the small pieces. They had hold of that big one. Dr. Smirke was halfway up the big trestle ladder at that end"—she pointed down the room—"with one end of the garland in his hand. Mrs. Smirke was just starting up the ladder at this end. I said, 'Shall I hold the ladder?' But she replied, 'It's quite firm. Will you go into the middle of the room and raise the big garland in your hands? It will make it easier for us to draw it up.' I raised it; it was quite light, as you'll see, but, of course, very awkward to handle. Mrs. Smirke couldn't quite get it to come up with her. They asked me to raise my part as high as I could. I did, and then heard Mrs. Smirke say, 'I can't quite bring it up far enough.' Then he said, 'Look, Marion, if you bend down, now you're near the top, bring your head down till it's just by the top step, as I'm doing, you'll be able to keep your balance and stretch a little further. But keep your head close in to the ladder.' I could see her, through the swath of leaves I was holding shoulder-high, bend over easily in the way he told her and stretch out. I stood on tiptoe. But it was no use. She couldn't make the cord come any further. I suppose the whole long garland was heavier than it looked, and she hadn't an overfirm position. But she wasn't nervous; quite sure of herself. She called out, 'Either it's caught at your end, or Mary can't raise it high enough.' 'It's not caught here,' he called back. 'It must need more raising in the middle. We'll have to wait. I expect the guests tonight won't mind helping us. 'Thank you, Mary,' they both said, and I waited until they were down; we let the big garland rest on the ground, and I followed them back into the house."

"Well, thank you, Mary," both the men repeated. She smiled and went out.

"Nothing premeditated there," remarked the Sergeant as the door closed. "You see, they were going to have raised that garland themselves that afternoon, with Mary to help. I'd thought possibly he might have planned the fall as an after-dinner effort. They had quite a little wine at the meal. But in the afternoon they'd had nothing, and it was only when they couldn't get it fixed themselves that they thought of trying to do it after dinner with the guests' help."

"That is one line," said the Doctor.

"Do you mean that you see another?"

"Perhaps, but I own I can't pull on it yet. Who else in the house?"

"There's the furnace man."

"Let's have him up."

The Sergeant was back in a moment with a quiet, elderly man. "Can you, Mr. Calkin," the Sergeant said when they had seated him, "help us in forming a picture of what led up to the accident?"

The man reflected for a while. The only sound was his calloused hand passing over a day's strong gray stubble on his chin. Then he cleared his throat.

"Of course, you gentlemen mean they weren't getting on. I suppose most people in the know knew that. No, they weren't. But you don't want my opinions." He rose and went toward the studio door.

"Here!" exclaimed the Sergeant.

"No, out here," came the reply.

"A good witness," said Dr. Wendover, following Calkin. The Sergeant brought up the rear, first looking carefully around the room. That was part of his routine when anyone asked him to "change venue."

When he reached the doorway, Wendover and Calkin were already across the small yard toward the house. But they were not going into it, but under it.

Catching up, he heard Calkin saying, "I often sit down here a bit when I've set the furnace. It's warm and quiet—quieter than at home. I sit here and smoke by myself. The smoke goes up the flue. You don't hear any noises, not even from the house. There's nothing above here but a little lean-to place. Believe Dr. Smirke used it to do some of his dispensing and test work there before the big new lab in his new office uptown took care of all that for him. I suppose, because I knew it wasn't used, that I pricked up my ears one day, hearing someone moving overhead in it. Whoever was there, was there some time. For at last it was time for me to go back home after giving the old stove a final trim. As I turned around, letting myself out by that back gate, 'longside the studio, sure enough, I saw Dr. Smirke working away at what looked like a little tank near the window. Next day, as I went down these stairs, I glanced up at the window. Standing on the ledge—he shifted it after—there was a sort of little aquarium with a big shrimp or two in it. I got used to the doctor being in there. Don't know that I thought about it.

Have heard a man may like to do a bit of research without others knowing of it till he's ready to publish."

"Yes," agreed Dr. Wendover, "men have had their discoveries stolen."

"But one day I heard a second person come in, after he'd been working there quietly by himself some time. It was Mrs. Smirke. I heard her voice."

He rose and hit the plank roof. "You see, you couldn't fail. I didn't want to eavesdrop, but the storm broke straight away. Her 'What are you doing?' might have made a quieter man than Smirke ask her to mind her business. He didn't, though, break out of a sudden. Said something, as far as I could catch, about a piece of natural history research. She was silent a bit. I could hear her step coming across the room. She was evidently going closer, to see what he was up to. Then she practically broke out right over my head here. 'You're torturing the poor thing!' He growled back, 'Don't be a fool, Marion.' 'But look, it's lying on its side. It's dying.' 'Well, you're not a vegetarian!' She was very fond of her food, true enough, and a big eater. 'You've no right to torture a dumb beast for your beastly science.' 'I'm not torturing it,' he shouted back.

"By that time, as I couldn't get out and couldn't help hearing, I felt I couldn't do much harm if I saw as well as heard. I couldn't think what it was they were making all this row over." Calkin got up and moved to a further corner of the furnace catacomb.

"You see, if you stand on this step—it's the first of an old flight which used to lead into the house—you're raised up just where the floor above is raised too. Up there is the step which leads from the lean-to to the main house."

They followed him onto the stair and, through a crack in the joining, they saw straight onto the window ledge of the room above.

"That was just where the little tank was."

"Let's go up and have a close-up," said Dr. Wendover. In a minute the three of them were in the lean-to. The Sergeant and the Doctor turned at once to the window.

"Look, a small tank was fitted to here."

"Right enough," followed up the Sergeant, "there are the screw holes for the two brackets and the stains made by the water."

"There's been some other fitting here, though."

"Maybe, but one can't say what it was."

Just under the window frame it was difficult to see, but the Doctor, taking out a flashlight, threw a small circle of light on the wall.

"An electric wire was brought up this wall, just behind the tank."

"How do you know?"

"Look, do you see those two parallel dark bands like faint stains of soot? Well, they are the precipitation of dust and grime made by the induced current."

"And what does that show?"

"It means one more thread. But, as I've said, I don't want to pull on the string before it's woven."

Then, turning from Skillin to Calkin, "What else did you witness?"

"I own I was surprised. There they were quarreling over a

shrimp. The light from the window shone into the glass tank. They were standing each side of it, looking at it, and quite obviously at a big shrimp that was floating in it. 'It's only a little upset,' he remarked. Then I did notice that the shrimp was on its side, like fishes go when they're going to die. 'It's dying,' she cried. She was an excitable creature—that was the main reason that they couldn't get on. 'I tell you it's not; it's only a little upset and will be right in a jiffy.' With that, he put his hand behind the tank. There was a click and, by gum, I saw the queer little creature come right away onto an even keel. 'There,' he said, 'didn't I tell you you were wrong! Now, perhaps, in future you'll mind your own business.' "

"A fine piece of reporting, Mr. Calkin and, I believe, an illuminating bit of dialogue," remarked Dr. Wendover.

"Well, it only throws light on what we know already," joined in the Sergeant, "that they'd reached the point when they'd quarrel over anything."

"No," answered the Doctor, "no. I believe it shows that the crisis had gone further than that."

Then, turning to Calkin, "Did she say anything more?"

"Yes, she burst out again: 'You've hypnotized the poor creature.'

"He seemed caught between humor and rage. 'Marion,' he shouted, actually stamping the floor and sending a whiff of dust into my eyes. 'Don't be such a damned fool. You'll be thinking next that someone has been hexing you and that *you* can't walk straight.' 'I wouldn't put it past you. God, why didn't I marry a quiet straight fellow—?' She broke off, and he added, 'Like Gray?' And that suddenly calmed it. Some women are like dogs that way. There's a frightful roll-over of a fight, and you think there must be murder, and the puff-pastry flops."

"Thank you, Mr. Calkin, I think we have that situation plain."

When the furnaceman had gone and the two had returned to the studio, Dr. Wendover added, "A woman may forget, but a man remembers. Hell hath a worse fury than a woman scorned, and that's the cold rage of a man who wants a home and rest and understanding, and finds home is only an enclosure where fighting is without gloves or any rules of the game. Well, we certainly have a *casus belli.* Now, to make quite clear the plan of attack. Sergeant, would you send again for Mary the maid? I've got one more small investigation to do here."

The Sergeant was some time in fetching Mary. She had gone up to her room, to change before going out. When she and the Sergeant reached the studio, they found Dr. Wendover looking at the right-hand ladder. It lay like a Goliath at the feet of the small David who had brought it down and was closely examining its head.

"You're pretty nimble to heel over a temporary staircase like that," laughed Skillin.

"Oh, it's strong enough, but not really heavy. But it will rest for the moment. We mustn't keep you waiting, Mary. I see you were going out. I've only three or four questions more and then, I promise you, I've finished. We've been going back a bit, trying to think how this painful accident could have happened. Was your late mistress getting more—nervous?"

"Well, Doctor, you realize she was always irritable, quite excitable, you might say."

"Yes, but had it grown?"

"No, I'm sure it hadn't."

"But they had had—quarrels?"

"Oh, yes, but you know, Mrs. Smirke was that kind of lady that just can't help herself, and who says then that quarrels clear the air. They do with some people, and I believe she had a little sort of nerve irritation which made it worse. Anyhow, I'm sure they'd been better friends for some time. They'd had a bad break out in that little back room. I heard it. They made quite a noise, and I was washing up the table glasses in the back pantry. But after that they were on better terms. There's nothing like a little trouble for making one make up after a quarrel."

"What do you mean?"

"Well, it's not a very nice subject, but I think it may have had something to do with her temper, as I've said. . . ." She paused. "I hardly like to say. . . ."

"You are hardly likely to shock Sergeant Skillin or myself."

"Well, she had, poor lady, that kind of skin that needs a lot of care—too rich a skin. My face masseuse tells me the other little trouble goes with it. . . ." Then, with an effort of real relevation, "she had wax in the ears."

"We all have," replied Dr. Wendover reassuringly. "It's a very necessary protection for an organ which is very delicate, delicate enough to be shocked by a sound wave, and yet must be always open to dust and germs."

"Well," reasserted Miss Holster, "it's hardly nice, and she was naturally very sensitive about it, and it did annoy her, vex her. I'd see her struggle not to put her little finger in her ear."

"An ancient trouble, so ancient that that finger is called the ear finger."

Then, confirming the witness, the Doctor added, "And the wax can cause considerable irritation if it thickens, and if an unskillful nail works at it you have a good source of infection there."

"Well, she didn't like going to a strange doctor. So every few months Dr. Smirke would syringe it out for her. Often they'd start all right. But she *was* so sensitive and he was so irritable. She'd say he hurt her, and he'd say she was a cry-baby. I'd hear it often, for he'd call me in to bring the hot water and hold the towels and things. But the last time I was with them on it he was quite sympathetic. When she winced, I remember him saying in a really nice tone of voice—it surprised me a bit, so I remember it—'You're right, Marion, this time I think it really has caused a little real pruitis'—Is that the word?" Mary asked.

"Near enough, please go on."

"He looked in with a sort of instrument. Then he said, 'But I think I know what can settle the trouble for good.' Maybe a few days after, at table, he said, 'I've been making inquiries from colleagues. Their reports are very favorable. Come up to the office one day and have a few treatments with X rays on that spot in the ear, and I'll wager you'll never feel it again.' She was away a day and came back with a small dressing in the ear. I don't remember her complaining for another week. Then, one day at dinner, I saw her putting her hand up to her ear."

"Which?" asked Dr. Wendover.

"How'd a girl remember that?" grunted Sergeant Skillin.

"Oh, but I do. It was her right ear, the one which had been treated. For I remember she had on her fine ruby ring that she always wore on her right hand. I recall thinking how finely it flashed in the light of the candles."

"Did she say anything?" asked Dr. Wendover again.

"I remember, Dr. Smirke said, 'You're not feeling that ear again? The X ray is said to be a certain cure.' She only said something about it being a little numb. Then, later, she said something, too, about being so nervous that she was glad to have the anesthetic when he was giving her the X rays."

"Oh, she was thankful for having had an anesthetic?" interrupted Dr. Wendover.

"Yes, and she added, 'It's worth it to be rid of that horrid tickle.' I remember, because she wasn't the kind of person ever to notice things getting better but very quick to notice them if they were worse. I thought that tickle must have been pretty tough for someone to think it was worth a certain amount of trouble to be rid of it. Of course, she'd have to complain about the little numbness she felt in its place."

"Of course," said Dr. Wendover reflectively.

"Well, Doctor, that was all. A week after there was the accident."

Mary left, thanked and commiserated on loss of part of an afternoon. As her footsteps died away, Sergeant Skillin rose. "That closes the case. Those are the only 'on the spot' witnesses. The three couples of diners can't tell us anything more than they told at the inquest."

"I agree, I agree," said Dr. Wendover in a sort of perfunctory aside.

"Well, then, there's nothing more to do, is there?"

To that, there was not given even an inattentive assent. The Doctor continued gazing at the prone ladder, its long legs sprawled almost touching the wall on their right, its head now reaching a considerable way up the floor of the long room.

"After all, you can't reopen a case," the Sergeant called at him, "if all you can say for fact is that a violent-tempered unstable woman, after exasperating her husband, fell off the top of a tall ladder. To want a person dead isn't murder."

Dr. Wendover shifted around. "It is, morally."

"We're not Morality, we're Law."

"Um; it's a natural law that where there's a will there's a way."

"Well, the way was the ladder. How did he will her to fall off, and neatly, plumb on her head! He couldn't have pulled her off. Six people were on the line in between."

Dr. Wendover did not answer but turned back to looking at the ladder itself. Sergeant Skillin tried to rouse him:

"Why did you pull it down?"

"Why, it's our last witness."

"It'll tell us nothing we don't know. We know everyone who handled it. Doubt if you'd even find the poor woman's fingerprints on it."

Evidently no longer listening, the Doctor had strolled up to the ladder's head, where the hinged back-supports joined onto the top of the flight of steps. Sergeant Skillin was reaching the end of his tether.

"Here," he called out, excusing himself for his tone of voice—because old Wendover was really daydreaming—"if you want to interrogate that dumb scantling, you won't get anything from its head, from that old clotheshorse's mouth," he chuckled, his natural good temper restored by his own small joke. "Its feet, at my end, are the only thing that might help us. But, of course, I've questioned them."

He bent down and looked at the undersurfaces of the ladder's ends, now visible. "Y'see, as true and firm as you could wish or, rather, as we could not wish." He shook the ladder's struts and tried the steps. "No play there. These ladders are new and of good workmanship."

Dr. Wendover turned. "Then they were purchased lately."

"Yes, Dr. Smirke had bought them a couple of months ago. He told the man who provided them, and whom he'd dealt with for some years, that he was tired of those dangerous lean-to ladders and had nearly had an accident or two by their slipping on this smooth floor. This year, he said, he'd have safe ladders before he started decorations for the Christmas party. And they are safe."

The Doctor assented, "He was certainly a careful man." That did not, however, take his attention from the ladder head at his feet. Finally, as Sergeant Skillin was strolling to the door, he roused himself to call him back. "You said we shouldn't get anything from this old clotheshorse's mouth. I like your simile, but I venture to differ from you in your dismissal of this witness."

"Well, you'll have to do the translating and, remember, not to me, your indulgent friend, but to a court and an expensive defending lawyer."

"You'll at least let me rehearse the part in front of you."

"Oh, go ahead."

"First, be so kind as to bend yours a little, so that you may see the witness's mouth."

Sergeant Skillin did consent to bend his head sideways. "Why, that's only a handhold." Sure enough, just under the broad platform top-step, in the side piece of wood which supported it, a space was cut, big enough to put a hand through.

"And, look, there's the companion one on the other side." The Sergeant drew himself up, glad to counterquiz the Doctor. "They must be handholds for carrying the ladder."

"No; if the ladder was a four-foot one, instead of four times that height, you might carry it so. But, see, this big thing, if it is carried, must be carried longways; its weight would require two hands, and, then, if this is a handhold, it should be at right angles to the way it is actually cut. Besides, these cuts weren't made by the maker. That sawing isn't professional carpentry. That he troubled to paint over the cuts shows that he wished to hide his work as much as possible. Finally, the incision is right up under the top piece."

"Yes, but that doesn't hide it when you look up from the floor."

"It is in the shadow cast by the overlap of the board above. But he had a second reason for putting the opening as high as he could, his real reason. He needed it to be flush with the underside of the top board."

"But what about the other opening on the other side?"

"It's a blind."

"Oh, you can't get rid of additional facts that don't support your theory by dismissing them as lead-away false clues."

"Well, now we'll get to the center, and that will show.

We've simply been looking at the not very communicative mouth."

Dr. Wendover knelt down and the Sergeant followed suit. The pocket flashlight threw its bright circle on the underside of the top board of the ladder.

"Not much there." A grumbling tone was coming back into the Sergeant's voice. The bright circle traveled along the grain of the wood.

"Those little indentations," the Doctor's voice said beside him. "A couple here; another couple here; a third pair here; and now . . ." the light dipped down some four inches and retraced its course. "You see the same little indents and, now, as we reach the end, by what I have called the blind mouth on the ladder's right side, a final couple of these same small punctures."

"Well, there may have been some bit of upholstery or mat tacked onto the top step so you could kneel on it safely without danger of its slipping."

"Queer, then, that there is no pair of punctures on this left-hand side."

"Oh, this is altogether too fine-drawn, Doctor!"

"We are dealing with something very fine," he allowed, "but, really, no finer than a fingerprint. This is a very clear and telling impression."

As they rose from their knees and he slipped the torch back into his pocket, he took out a pad and pencil. "Let's chart those punctures like a graph." He plotted them on the paper. "See, they weren't quite parallel: while on the right side, where the two lines most diverged, they were closed by that last couple of indents and, on the left side, where they are closest, there is no closing brace of punctures." He rapidly drew connecting lines through the points he had plotted.

Sergeant Skillin, looking over his shoulder, remarked, "Well, they might be the marks of the tacks that held on a cloth cover, as I've said. You see, since the person was so unskillful as not to keep his lines straight, they'd diverged at the right side, so that he had to put in an extra pair of tacks."

"But if he wasn't unskillful?" asked Dr. Wendover. "If that design follows very carefully a pattern? Then, Skillin, does that pattern suggest anything to you?"

"It looks like an elongated horseshoe pointing to the left."

"Yes. And by your insight, by your reading the writing punctured on this panel, you have got your man."

Sergeant Skillin was quite pleased at the praise, even more doubtful of the statement, and completely puzzled at the demonstration. So he naturally said nothing.

"Yes," went on Dr. Wendover, stretching himself. "Take a chair, Sergeant. Thought contracts the muscles, do what we will. Well, it's over. We can relax. We've time. Smirke was so clever that he's quite at his ease. He won't move till you come for him, and then he'll go quiet, certain you can't know, or if you suspect, can't prove. All we have to do now, as I suspect you've seen through to the end, is to make certain that the jury has as clear a view as we. You're undoubtedly right-that almost-closed curve, plotted by those pairs of punctures on the underside of that top board of the ladder, are the print or outline of a horseshoe, or, if you like to put it in criminal-court language, of the weapon with which Mrs. Smirke was killed. And the small 'mouth' in that ladder's head, on its left side, is the gun port through which Mrs. Smirke was shot."

"Now, Doctor dear, do be sensible," broke in Sergeant Skillin. "With all yer blarney, ye know that I haven't the slightest idea of what ye are talking about. Glory be! The poor woman was *not* shot. Though she fell as though she had been."

"Sergeant, as always, you are right in what you observe, or have told you in evidence, but, being more used to courts than I, you sometimes fear to go as far as you really see. Mrs. Smirke was shot, shot in the ear."

"Sounds like *Hamlet* to me, and *Hamlet's* a good play but a bad crime story."

"You're right, then, we must have a little more proof."

"Can you get it?"

"I only want one piece more, literally a grain, to tip old justice's scales, even though they're rusty. And you can get it for me. We're too old hands to be upset by gruesome detail, you and I. Get me the right ear of the dead woman. I must have the real ear. The outer part doesn't matter."

"It'll need going through a few forms, you know?"

"Well, again I wager we have time. What we're looking for will keep."

Sergeant Skillin was impressed. That ladder had been tampered with, carefully, queerly and, further, he knew Mrs. Smirke's ear had been doctored by a doctor who did not wish her well. Had the ladder top on the night of the murder held the key? He did not like to think he might have overlooked that. Could the dead woman's ear be the lock that key fitted in? "I'll get it for you," he said.

He had only to get the papers through. Dr. Wendover and the police surgeon managed the anatomical side between them. Within twenty-four hours he received a call from the Doctor's house, asking him to come over. He was taken at once to the Doctor's private laboratory at the top of the house. As soon as he entered he saw a microscope standing under a high light and he noticed, pointing at the specimen platform, an electrical rig-up of some sort.

"Sergeant, will you please look down that microscope?" were the Doctor's first words.

Silently, Sergeant Skillin took his place on the stool and peered down into the lit field. The Doctor's voice at his shoulder said, "What you are now observing is some fluid from the semicircular canal of the dead woman's ear. It is, of course, not very clear. The only definite things are some tiny black spots."

"I see them," reported the Sergeant.

"Keep your eye on them."

He heard a switch click, and exclaimed, "Oh, the small black spots have rushed ahead!"

The Doctor's voice at his shoulder said, "There, that's all; that's my final demonstration."

"But what is it at all?"

"Well, first, what did I do? I switched on a magnet. What followed? The black grains rushed toward it. What, therefore, are they? Minute steel dust, rustless steel. Where do they come from? The right inner ear of Mrs. Smirke, deceased. What would they do there when she was alive?" He paused.

The Sergeant hesitated, "How would I know?"

"You do know," the Doctor continued. "They would be in the fluid of her semicircular canals, or one of them. They wouldn't corrode—they are, as we surgeons say, 'inert'—they won't set up any *chemical* reaction. They, therefore, would do her no harm. They wouldn't upset her. She'd probably hardly know she was wearing such a strange interior decoration until—until she should, by chance, bring that right ear within an inch or so of a fairly strong magnet."

"God have mercy on us," remarked Sergeant Skillin with some conviction.

"Then she would be seized with violent, irresistible vertigo. Wherever she was, however securely placed, she would have to fall headlong."

"But how in heaven's name did the fellow find out the diabolical device?"

"Do you remember Calkin's story about the quarrel he overheard—and underlooked?"

"In the lean-to room back there?"

"Yes, with the little aquarium by the window."

"A quarrel over a shrimp!"

"No; a little more than a shrimp and, as it happens, considerably more significant—a crayfish, to be crustaceanly accurate."

"Well, what does it matter?—she was crazy anyhow and would have blown up over anything."

"But he wasn't. It was the crayfish which gave him his big idea and gave me the clue to what that idea was. I even wonder," he reflected, "whether the wretched woman's outburst, which seemed so absurd, may not have sprung from some deep subconscious sense that he was her enemy and, under the guise of some simple research, was seeking for a way to be rid of her."

"That's speculation," corrected Sergeant Skillin. "We've quite enough odd facts to order, without adding any theories. What makes you think that the crayfish gave him an idea—and you a clue?"

"Do you remember," questioned back the Doctor, "that we found traces that a fairly high voltage wire had been brought up just behind the tank, but not high enough to serve for a lamp above it. That wire served as an electrical magnet."

"How do you know?"

"Because of the way, according to Calkin's report, Mrs. Smirke spoke of the crayfish's behavior and of how he himself saw it behaving."

"That's true; he saw it on its side, 'like a dying fish,' and heard her scream at him that he was torturing it."

"And then, you recall, it suddenly righted itself."

"That was the moment Smirke put his hand behind the tank."

"That's it, and that's why. He switched off the magnet."

"But still. . . ."

"Yes," the Doctor said meditatively, "Smirke's daring thing was to carry over the experiment from fish to man—or woman. For there has been an odd discovery, known for some time, that crayfish balance themselves in the water by a small level in their heads. And when they molt their shells, they themselves actually replace small sand grains in the head, so that the touch of these gives them their poise—as the tipping of the liquid in our semicircular canals gives us our sense of balance. Not long ago it occurred to a researcher to give this crustacean iron filings, instead of ordinary sand, at the time of its shell-casting. Then, when they were all sealed up again in their new shells, he directed the current of a magnet through the water. At once all the crayfish within the field careened at right angles to the earth's gravitational field—but, of course, felt all right. They were straight and on the level with the main pull—that of the magnet. What they felt about it, however, need not, I think, concern us. After all, you are fairly safe whichever way you are up, if you are a fish in water. But . . ." he paused, "I still think the poor woman was right to feel alarmed at what she saw in that little pool. Like a witch looking into a crystal, she was seeing in symbolic form her own fate pre-enacted."

"But how the devil did he maneuver everything else?"

"He took his time. He is a cool man. Most murderers, as we know, spoil a good idea by rushing it, by not waiting to bring up enough supports. You remember, he first becomes considerate about her ear irritation. For then he could be considerate, since he had heard of the crayfish peculiarity, and a black hope was rising on the horizon of his mind. He would be patient, for his own irritation would not last much longer. When he looked into her ear with the auriscope"—

"Then the devil whispered into his," broke in the Sergeant.

"I prefer Shakespeare," resumed the Doctor. "'Oh! opportunity, thy guilt is great.' The two things, her ear and the crayfish fact coming together, made him feel he must dare it now. There was, no doubt, incipient pruritis in the middle ear. It's a vexing thing, especially in a nervous person. What's more terribly to the point, it's a condition very easy to inflame. No doubt he did so under the excuse of easing it, and then suggested a small treatment to soothe what he had made acute. Of course, when he gave her the anesthetic for the pretended X ray he made the incision and insertion. Very, very risky, but the devil often helps those he wishes to hang."

"Yes, I see the rest. He let the place heal and cured the pruritis properly, and then?"

"Why, then he maneuvered for position. The mine was loaded. Now he must fire it—or make her fire it. The steps are —the ladder she is to mount to help the Christmas decorations. It is loaded with a strong 'permanent' magnet, the ends of which come just to the opening under the top step on the left side. Then comes the rehearsal. He is careful enough for the afternoon trial with the maid Mary. He certainly did not want to bring off his grand slam then, with only one witness. He had six, all chosen. The magnet would then not be in place. He fixed it in its catches between that trial and the dinner hour. With a terrible detachment, he was teaching his victim to play her part—to know exactly how to mount the scaffold and put her head precisely where he could fell her as though with an executioner's ax. Yes, he was patient, resourceful, ready. If he failed on the night of the party, if she fell and didn't die, or didn't fall, he could try and try again, planting magnets and luring her within range, so that she would have falls that could prove fatal. We know he had taken care to tell her that she would next think that he had been hexing her. So, if she felt that at times she was losing control of herself, she would hesitate to consult another doctor. Violent-tempered people often fear that their lack of self control may mean that they may go mad. They fear it greatly, though, of course they are not the sort that do. Neurosis is not often the path to true madness." He paused again.

"Is that all? Of course, it's enough, the case is clear."

The Sergeant waited for a moment, for it seemed Dr. Wendover might still have something more to say. He had.

"It is a complete case," he said slowly. "I believe I can even now interpret the poor woman's last word."

"You mean what Mrs. Gortch thought she heard her say?"

"Yes, as she felt herself suddenly whirled around on her axis and knew that she must crash, I believe that the scene which had so irrationally but deeply stirred her flashed into her poor panic-stricken brain. She saw why she had been horrified by her husband's small piece of abstract research. She wasn't trying to say 'Gray.' Her last gasping word was, 'The CRAYfish.' "

THE GREAT FOG

The first symptom was a mildew.

Very few people have ever looked carefully at such "molds"; indeed, only a specialized branch of botanists knows about them. Nor is this knowledge—except rarely—of much use. Every now and then a low growth of this sort may attack a big cash crop. Then the mycologists, whose lifework is to study these spore growths, are called in by the growers. These botanists can sometimes find another mold which will eat its fellow. That closes the matter. The balance of life, which had been slightly upset, has been righted. It is not a matter of any general interest.

This particular mildew did not seem to have even that special importance. It did not, apparently, do any damage to the trees on which it grew. Indeed, most fruit growers never noticed it. The botanists found it themselves; no one called their attention to it. It was simply a form of spore growth different in its growth rate from any previously recorded. It did not seem to do any harm to any other form of life. But it did do amazingly well for itself. It was not a new plant, but a plant with quite a new power of growth.

It was this fact which puzzled the botanists, or rather that special branch of the botanists, the mycologists. That was why they finally called in the meteorologists. They asked for "another opinion," as baffled doctors say. What made the mycologists choose the meteorologists for consultation was this: Here was a mildew which spread faster than any other mold had ever been known to grow. It flourished in places where such mildews had been thought incapable of growing. But there seemed to be no botanical change either in the mold or in the plants it grew on. Therefore the cause must be climatic: only a weather change could account for the unprecedented growth.

The meteorologists saw the force of this argument. They became interested at once. The first thing to do, they said, was to study the mildew, not as a plant, but as a machine, an indicator. "You know," said Sersen the weatherman to Charles the botanist (they had been made colleagues for the duration of the study), "the astronomers have a thing called a thermocouple that will tell the heat of a summer day on the equator of Mars. Well, here is a little gadget I've made. It's almost as sensitive to damp as the thermocouple is to heat."

Sersen spent some time rigging it up and then "balancing" it, as he called it. "Find the normal humidity and then see how much the damp at a particular spot exceeds that." But he went on fiddling about far longer than Charles thought an expert who was handling his own gadget should. He was evidently puzzled. And after a while he confessed that he was.

"Queer, very queer," said Sersen. "Of course, I expected to get a good record of humidity around the mold itself. As you say, it can't grow without that: it wouldn't be here unless the extra damp was here too. But, look here," he said, pointing to a needle that quivered near a high number on a scale.

"*That* is the humidity actually around the mold itself—what we might expect, if a trifle high. That's not the surprise. It's *this.*" He had swung the whole instrument on its tripod until it pointed a foot or more from the mold; for the tree they were studying was a newly attacked one and, as far as Charles had been able to discover, had on it only this single specimen of the mildew.

Charles looked at the needle. It remained hovering about the high figure it had first chosen. "Well?" he queried.

"Don't you see?" urged Sersen. "This odd high humidity is present not only around the mold itself but for more than a foot beyond."

"I don't see much to that."

"I see two things," snapped Sersen; "one's odd; the other's damned odd. The odd one anyone not blind would see. The other one is perhaps too big to be seen until one can stand well back."

"Sorry to be stupid," said Charles, a gentle-spoken but close-minded little fellow; "we botanists are small-scale men."

"Sorry to be a snapper," apologized Sersen. "But, as I suppose you've guessed, I'm startled. I've got a queer feeling that we're on the track of something big, yes, and something maybe moving pretty fast. The first odd thing isn't a complete surprise: it's that you botanists have shown us what could turn out to be a meteorological instrument more delicate and more accurate than any we have been able to make. Perhaps we ought to have been on the outlook for some such find. After all, living things are always the most sensitive detectors—can always beat mechanical instruments when they want to. You know about the mitogenetic rays given out by breeding seeds. Those rays can be recorded only by yeast cells—which multiply rapidly when exposed to the rays, thus giving an indication of their range and strength."

"Umph," said Charles. Sersen's illustration had been unfortunate, for Charles belonged to that majority of conservative botanists to whom the mitogenetic radiation was mere moonshine.

Sersen, again vexed, went on: "Well, whether you accept them or not, I still maintain that here we have a superdetector. This mildew can notice an increase in humidity long before any of our instruments. There's proof that something has changed in the climate. This mold is the first to know about it—and to profit by it. I prophesy it will soon be over the whole world."

"But your second discovery, or supposition?" Charles had no use for prophecy. These weathermen, he thought; well, after all, they aren't quite scientists, so one mustn't blame them, one supposes, for liking forecasts—forecasting is quite unscientific.

Charles was a courteous man, but Sersen was sensitive. "Well," he said defensively, "that's nothing but supposition." And yet, he thought to himself as he packed up his instrument, if it *is* true it may mean such a change that botany will be blasted and meteorology completely mistified. His small private joke relieved his temper. By the time they returned to headquarters he and Charles were friendly enough. They agreed to make a joint report which would stick severely to the facts.

Meanwhile, botanists everywhere were observing and recording the spreading of the mildew. Before long, they began to get its drift. It was spreading from a center, spreading like a huge ripple from where a stone has been flung into a lake. The center, there could be no doubt, was eastern Europe. Spain, Britain, and North Africa showed the same "high incidence." France showed an even higher one. The spread of the mold could be watched just as well in North or South America. Such and such a percentage of shrubs and trees was attacked on the Atlantic coasts; a proportionately lower percentage on the Pacific coasts; but everywhere the incidence was rising. On every sector of the vast and widening circle, America, Africa, India, the mildew was advancing rapidly.

Sersen continued his own research on the mold itself, on the "field of humidity" around each plant. He next made a number of calculations correlating the rapid rate of dispersal, the average increase of infestation of all vegetation by the mold, and the degree of humidity which must result. Then, having checked and counterchecked, at last he was ready to read his paper and give his conclusions at a joint meeting of the plant men and the weathermen.

Just before Sersen went up to the platform, he turned to Charles. "I'm ready now to face the music," he said, "because I believe we are up against something which makes scientific respectability nonsense. We've got to throw caution aside and tell the world." "That's serious," said Charles cautiously. "It's damned serious," said Sersen, and went up the steps to the rostrum.

When he came down, the audience was serious too; for a moment, as serious as he. He had begun by showing the world map with its spreading, dated lines showing where the mildew in its present profusion had reached; showing also where, in a couple of months, the two sides of the ripple would meet. Soon, almost every tree and shrub throughout the world would be infested, and, of course, the number of molds per tree and bush would increase. That was interesting and queer, but of no popular concern. The molds still remained harmless to their tree hosts and to animal life—indeed, some insects seemed rather happy about the botanical change. As far, then, as the change was only a change in mildew reproduction there was no cause for much concern, still less for alarm. The mold had gone ahead, because it was the first to benefit from some otherwise undetectable change in climate. The natural expectation would, then, be that insects, the host plants, or some other species of mold would in turn advance and so readjust the disturbed balance of nature.

But that was only the first part of Sersen's lecture. At that phrase, "balance of nature," he paused. He turned from the world map with its charting of the mold's growth. For a moment he glanced at another set of statistical charts; then he seemed to change his mind and touched the buzzer. The lights went out, and the beam from the stereoptican shot down through the darkened hall. The lighted screen showed a tree; on its branches and trunk a number of red crosses had been marked. Around each cross was a large circle, so large that some of the circles intersected.

"Gentlemen," said Sersen, "this is the discovery that really matters. Until now, perhaps unwisely, I have hesitated to communicate it. That the mold spreads, you know. That it is particularly sensitive to some otherwise undetected change in the weather, you know. Now, you must know a third fact about it—it is a weather *creator*. Literally, it can brew a climate of its own.

"I have proved that in each of these circles—and I am sure they are spreading circles—the mold is going far to create its own peculiar atmosphere—a curiously high and stable humidity. The statistically arranged readings which I have prepared, and which I have here, permit, I believe, of no other conclusion. I would also add that I believe we can see why this has happened. It is now clear what permitted this unprecedented change to get under way. We have pulled the trigger that has fired this mine. No doubt the mold first began to increase because a slight change in humidity helped it. But now it is—how shall I put it—co-operating. It is *making the humidity increase*.

"There has probably been present, these past few years, one of those small increases in atmospheric humidity which occur periodically. In itself, it would have made no difference to our lives and, indeed, would have passed unperceived. But it was at this meteorological moment that European scientists began to succeed in making a new kind of quick-growing mold which could create fats. It is, perhaps, the most remarkable of all the war efforts, perhaps the most powerful of all the new defensive weapons—against a human enemy. But in regard to the extra human world in which we live it may prove as dangerous as a naked flame in a mine chamber filled with firedamp. For, need I remind you, molds are spore-reproducing growths. Fungus is by far the strongest form of life. It breeds incessantly and will grow under conditions no other form of life will endure. When you play with spore life you may at any moment let loose something the sheer power of which makes dynamite look like a damp squib. I believe what man has now done is precisely that—he has let the genie out of its bottle, and we may find ourselves utterly helpless before it."

Sersen paused. The lights came on. Dr. Charles rose and caught the chairman's eye. Dr. Charles begged to state on behalf of the botanical world that he hoped Dr. Sersen's dramatic remarks would not be taken gravely by the press or the public. Dr. Sersen had spoken of matters botanical. Dr. Charles wished to say that he and his colleagues had had the mildew under protracted observation. He could declare categorically that it was not dangerous.

Sersen had not left the platform. He strode back to the rostrum. "I am not speaking as a botanist," he exclaimed, "I am speaking as a meteorologist. I have told you of what I am sure—the balance of life has been upset. You take for granted that the only balance is life against life, animal against animal, vegetable against vegetable. You were right to call in a weatherman, but that's of no use unless you understand what he is telling you."

The audience shifted offendedly in its seats. It wasn't scientific to be as urgent as all that. Besides, hadn't Charles said there was no danger? But what was their queer guest now saying?

"I know, every meteorologist knows, that this nature-balance is far vaster and more delicately poised than you choose to suspect. All life is balanced against its environment. Cyclones are brought on, climate can change, a glacial age can begin as the result of atmospheric alterations far too small for the layman to notice. In our atmosphere, that wonderful veil and web under which we are sheltered and in which we grow, we have a condition of extraordinary delicacy. The right—or rather the precisely wrong—catalytic agent can send the whole thing suddenly into quite another arrangement, one which can well be desperately awkward for man. It has taken an amazing balance of forces to allow human beings to live. That's the balance you've upset. Look out."

He studied his audience. There they sat, complacent, assured, only a little upset that an overexcitable colleague should be behaving unscientifically—hysterically, almost. Suddenly, with a shock of despair, Sersen realized that it was no use hoping to stir these learned experts. These were the actual minds which had patiently, persistently, purblindly worked the very changes which must bring the house down on their heads. They'd never asked, never wished to ask, what might be the general and ultimate effects of their burrowing. We're just another sort of termite, thought Sersen, as he looked down on the rows of plump faces and dull-ivory-colored pates. We tunnel away trying to turn everything into "consumable goods" until suddenly the whole structure of things collapses round us.

He left the rostrum, submitted to polite thanks, and went home. A week later his botanical hosts had ceased even to talk about his strange manners. Hardly anyone else heard of his speech.

The first report of trouble—or rumor rather (for such natural-history notes were far too trivial to get into the battle-crammed papers)—came from orchard growers in deep valleys. Then fruit growers began to gossip when the Imperial Valley, hot and dry as hell, began to report much the same thing. It was seen at night at the start and cleared off in the day; so it seemed no more than an odd, inconsequent little phenomenon. But if you went out at full moon you did see a queer sight. Every tree seemed to have a sort of iridescent envelope, a small white cloud or silver shroud all its own.

Of course, soon after that, the date growers had something to howl about. The dates wouldn't stand for damp—and each silver shroud was, for the tree about which it hung, a vapor bath. But the date growers, all the other growers decided, were done for anyway; they'd have made a howl in any case when the new Colorado water made the irrigation plans complete. The increase in humidity would inevitably spoil their crop when the valley became one great oasis.

The botanists didn't want to look into the matter again. Botanically, it was uninteresting. The inquiry had been officially closed. But the phenomenon continued to be noticed farther and farther afield.

The thing seemed then to reach a sort of saturation point. A new sort of precipitation took place. The cloud around each tree and bush, which now could be seen even during the day, would, at a certain moment, put out feeler-like wisps and join up with the other spreading and swelling ground clouds stretching out from the neighboring trees. Sersen, who had thrown up his official job just to keep track of this thing, described that critical night when, with a grim prophetic pleasure, he saw his forecast fulfilled before his eyes. His last moldering papers have remained just decipherable for his great-grandchildren.

"I stood," he said, "on a rock promontory south of Salton Sea. The full moon was rising behind me and lighted the entire Valley. I could see the orchards glistening, each tree surrounded by its own cloud. It was like a gargantuan dew; each dew-globule tree-size. And then, as I watched, just like a great tide, an obliterating flood of whiteness spread over everything. The globules ran into one another until I was looking down on a solid sea of curd-white, far denser than mist or fog. It looked as firm, beautiful, and dead as the high moon which looked down on it. 'A new Deluge,' I said to myself. 'May I not ask who has been right? Did I not foretell its coming and did not I say that man had brought it on his own head?' "

Certainly Sersen had been justified. For, the morning after his vigil, when the sun rose, the Fog did not. It lay undisturbed, level, dazzling white as a sheet of snow-covered ice, throwing back into space every ray of heat that fell on it. The air immediately above it was crystal clear. The valley was submerged under an element that looked solid enough to be walked on. The change was evidently so complete because it was a double one, a sudden reciprocal process. All the damp had been gathered below the Fog's surface, a surface as distinct as the surface of water. Conversely, all the cloud, mist, and aqueous vapor in the air above the Fog was evidently drained out of it by this new dense atmosphere. It was as though the old atmosphere had been milk. The mold acted as a kind of rennet, and so, instead of milk, there remained only this hard curd and the clear whey. The sky above the Fog was not so much the deepest of blues—it was almost a livid black; the sun in it was an intense, harsh white and most of the big stars were visible throughout the day. So, outside the Fog it was desperately cold. At night it was agonizingly so. Under that cold the Fog lay packed dense like a frozen drift of snow.

Beneath the surface of the Fog, conditions were even stranger. Passing into it was like going suddenly into night. All lights had to be kept on all day. But they were not much use. As in a bad old-fashioned fog, but now to a far worse degree, the lights would not penetrate the air. For instance, the rays of a car's headlights formed a three-foot cone, the base of which looked like a circular patch of light thrown on an opaque white screen. It was possible to move about in the Fog, but only at a slow walking pace—otherwise you kept running into things. It was a matter of groping about, with objects suddenly looming up at you—the kind of world in which a severe myopic case must live if he loses his spectacles.

Soon, of course, people began to notice with dismay the Fog's effect on crops and gardens, on houses and goods. Nothing was ever again dry. Objects did not become saturated, but they were, if at all absorbent, thoroughly damp. Paper molded, wood rotted, iron rusted. But concrete, glass, pottery, all stone ware and ceramics remained unaffected. Cloth, too, served adequately, provided the wearer could stand its never being dry.

The first thought in the areas which had been first attacked was, naturally, to move out. But the Fog moved too. Every night some big valley area suddenly "went over." The tree fog around each tree would billow outward, join up with all its fellows, and so make a solid front and surface. Then came the turn for each fog-submerged valley, each fog-lake, to link with those adjacent to it. The general level of these lakes then rose. Instead of there being, as until now, large flooded areas of lowland, but still, in the main, areas of clear upland, this order was now reversed. The mountain ranges had become strings of islands which emerged from a shining ocean that covered the whole earth's surface, right up to the six-thousand-foot level.

Any further hope of air travel was extinguished. In the Fog, lack of visibility, of course, made it impossible. Above the Fog, you could see to the earth's edge: the horizons, cleared of every modulation of mist, seemed so close that you would have thought you could have touched them with your hand. As far as sight was concerned, above the Fog, near and far seemed one. But even if men could have lived in that thin air and "unscreened" light, no plane could be sustained by it.

Sea travel was hardly more open. True, the surface of the oceans lay under the Fog-blanket, as still as the water, a thousand fathoms down. But on that oily surface—that utterly featureless desert of motionless water—peering man, only a few yards from the shore, completely lost his way. Neither sun nor stars ever again appeared over the sea to give him his bearings. So man soon abandoned the sea beyond the closest inshore shallows. Even if he could have seen his way over the ocean, he could not have taken it. There was never a breath of wind to fill a sail, and the fumes from any steamship or motorboat would have hung around the vessel and would have almost suffocated the crew.

Retreat upward was cut off. For when the Fog stabilized at six thousand feet, it was no use thinking of attempting to live above it. Even if the limited areas could have given footing, let alone feeding, to the fugitive populations, no hope lay in that direction. For the cold was now so intense above the Fog that no plant would grow. And, worse, it was soon found, to the cost of those who ventured out there, that through this unscreened air—air which was so thin that it could scarcely be breathed—came also such intense ultraviolet radiations from the sun and outer space that a short exposure to them was fatal.

So the few ranges and plateaus which rose above the six-thousand-foot level stood gaunt as the ribs of a skeleton carcass under the untwinkling stars and the white glaring sun. After a very few exploratory expeditions out into that open, men realized that they must content themselves with a subsurface life, a new kind of fish existence, nosing about on the floor of a pool which henceforth was to be their whole world. It might be a poor, confined way of living, but above that surface was death. A few explorers returned, but, though fish taken out of water may recover if put back soon enough, every above-the-Fog explorer succumbed from the effect. After a few days the lesions and sores of bad X-ray burning appeared. If, after that, the nervous system did not collapse, the wretched man literally began to fall to pieces.

Underneath the Fog-blanket men painfully, fumblingly worked out a new answer to living. Of course, it had to be done without preparation, so the cost was colossal. All who were liable to rheumatic damage and phthisis died off. Only a hardy few remained. Man had been clever enough to pull down the atmosphere-roof which had hung so loftily over his head, but he never learned again how to raise a cover as high, spacious, and pleasant as the sky's blue dome. The dividing out of the air was a final precipitation, a nonreversible change-down toward the final entropy. Man might stay on, but only at the price of being for the rest of his term on earth confined under a thick film of precipitated air. Maybe, even if he had been free and had had the power to move fast and see far, it would have been too great a task for him to have attempted to "raise the air." As he now found himself, pinned under the collapse he had caused, he had not a chance of even beginning to plan such a vast reconstruction.

His job, then, was just to work at making lurking livable. And, within the limits imposed, it was not absolutely impossible. True, all his passion for speed and travel and seeing far and quick, all that had to go. He who had just begun to feel that it was natural to fly, now was confined not even to the pace of a brisk walk but to a crawl. It was a life on the lowest gear. Of course, great numbers died just in the first confusion, when the dark came on, before the permanent change in humidity and light swept off the other many millions who could not adapt themselves. But, after a while, not only men's health but their eyes became adapted to the perpetual dusk. They began to see that the gloom was not pitch-dark. Gradually, increasing numbers learned to be able to go about without lamps. Indeed, they found that they saw better if they cultivated this "nightsight," this ancient part of the eye so long neglected by man when he thought he was master of things. They were greatly helped also by a type of faint phosphorescence, a "cold-light," which (itself probably another mold-mutation) appeared on most surfaces if they were left untouched, and so outlined objects with faint, ghostly high-lights.

So, as decentralized life worked itself out, men found that they had enough. War was gone, so that huge social hemorrhage stopped. Money went out of gear, and so that odd strangle hold on goods-exchange was loosed. Men just couldn't waste what they had, so they found they had much more than they thought. For one reason, it wasn't worth hoarding anything, holding back goods, real, edible, and wearable goods, for a rise in price. They rotted. The old medieval epitaph proved itself true in this new dark age: "What I spent I had: what I saved I lost." Altogether, life became more immediate and, what people had never suspected, more real because less diffused. It was no use having a number of things which had been thought to be necessities. Cars? You could not see to travel at more than four miles an hour, and not often at that. Radios? They just struck; either insulation against the damp was never adequate or the electric conditions, the radio-resonant layers of the upper atmosphere, had been completely altered. A wailing static was the only answer to any attempt to re-establish wireless communication.

It was a low-built, small-housed, pedestrian world. Even horses were too dashing; and they were blinder in the Fog than were men. As for your house, you could seldom see more than its front door. Metal was little used. Smelting it was troublesome (the fumes could hardly get away and nearly suffocated everyone within miles of a furnace), and when you got your iron and steel it began rusting at once. Glass knives were used instead. They were very sharp. Men learned again, after tens of thousands of years of neglect, how to flake flints, crystal, and all the silica rocks to make all manner of neat, sharp tools.

Man's one primary need, which had made for nearly all his hoarding, the animal craving to accumulate food stocks, that fear which, since the dawn of civilization, has made his granaries as vast as his fortresses, this need, this enemy, was wiped out by another freak botanical by-product of the Fog. The curious sub-fog climate made an edible fungus grow. It was a sort of manna. It rotted if you stored it. But it grew copiously everywhere, of itself. Indeed, it replaced grass: wherever grass had grown the fungus grew. Eaten raw, it was palatable and highly nutritious—more tasty and more wholesome than when cooked (which was a blessing in itself, since all fires burnt ill and any smoke was offensive in the dense air). Man, like the fishes, lived in a dim but fruitful element.

The mean temperature under the Fog stayed precisely at 67 degrees Fahrenheit, owing, evidently, to some basic balance, like that which keeps the sea below a certain depth always at 36 degrees, four degrees above freezing. Men, then, were never cold.

They stayed mainly at home, around their small settlements. What was the use of going about? All you needed and could use was at your door. There was nothing to see—your view was always limited to four feet. There was no use in trying to seize someone else's territory. You all had the same: you all had enough.

Art, too, changed. The art of objects was gone. So a purer, less collectible art took its place. Books would not last; and so memory increased enormously, and men carried their libraries in their heads—a cheaper way and much more convenient. As a result, academic accuracy, the continual quoting of authorities, disappeared. A new epic age resulted. Men in the dusk composed, extemporized, jointly developed great epics, sagas, and choruses, which grew like vast trees, generation after generation, flowering, bearing fruit, putting out new limbs. And, as pristine, bardic poetry returned, it united again with its nursery foster-brother, music. Wood winds and strings were ruined by the damp. But stone instruments, like those used by the dawn cultures, returned—giving beautiful pure notes. An orchestra of jade and marble flutes, lucid gongs, crystal-clear xylophones grew up. Just as the Arabs, nomads out on the ocean of sand, had had no plastic art, but, instead, a wonderful aural art of chant and singing verse, so the creative power of the men of the Umbral Epoch swung over from eye to ear. Indeed, the thick air which baffled the eye made fresh avenues and extensions for the ear. Men could hear for miles: their ears grew as keen as a dog's. And with this keenness went subtlety. They appreciated intervals of sound which to the old men of the open air would have been imperceptible. Men lived largely for music and felt they had made a good exchange when they peered at the last moldering shreds of pictorial art.

"Yes," said Sersen's great-grandson, when the shock of the change was over and mankind had accustomed itself to its new conditions, "yes, I suspect we were not fit for the big views, the vast world into which the old men tumbled up. It was all right to give animal men the open. But, once they had got power without vision, then either they had to be shut up or they would have shot and bombed everything off the earth's surface. Why, they were already living in tunnels when the Fog came. And out in the open, men, powerful as never before, nevertheless died by millions, died the way insects used to die in a frost, but died by one another's hands. The plane drove men off the fields. That was the thing, I believe, that made Mind decide we were not fit any longer to be at large. We were going too fast and too high to see what we were actually doing. So, then, Mind let man fancy that all he had to do was to make food apart from the fields. That was the Edible Mold, and that led straight, as my great-grandfather saw, to the atmospheric upset, the meteorological revolution. It really was a catalyst, making the well-mixed air, which we had always taken for granted as the only possible atmosphere, divide out into two layers as distinct as water and air. We're safer as we are. Mind knew that, and already we are better for our Fog cure, though it had to be drastic.

"Perhaps, one day, when we have learned enough, the Fog will lift, the old high ceiling will be given back to us. Once more Mind may say: 'Try again. The Second Flood is over. Go forth and replenish the earth, and this time remember that you are all one.' Meanwhile I'm thankful that we are as we are."

WINGLESS VICTORY

I WAS LOOKING for copy—"Moby Dick"stuff. I'm a "descriptive journalist." Now that whaling is about to join Purchas' *Pilgrims* and El Dorado hunting, I thought the time had come to "meet the last whalers." I've landed something, but whether it's a whale of a story or simply a snark, I can't make up my mind. As a yarn it's straight stuff, simple narrative. But the narrator. . . ?

There's a small public house near Wapping Stairs where old "masters" will drop in if they're on the Thames. That was the place where I used to go angling for whale stories. I own I'd found pretty well nothing. Even before it ceased to pay well, whaling was really large-scale knacking, butchery. That evening no one who'd actually ever smelled blubber had come in, and the few clients had all gone except one man. I'd come to the conclusion that my search was no good and that I'd better think up some other subject for a write-up. Certainly the last hanger-on in that doleful little bar looked a very unlikely source for a story. It was clear he wasn't a "master" of anything. Then something made me look at him twice. He was a lightly built fellow, pretty obviously down and out. But in some odd way, in spite of the air of wastrel and flotsam which his clothes and carriage pretty clearly bespoke, there was one little oddity that didn't fall in with the commonplace formula of failure, and, though it was a small thing, it caught my attention. It was a small thing but it was odd in such a make-up. It was his complexion.

Shabby and shambling as he was, he ought to have been withered and ill-colored. He wasn't. Out of his sordid suit emerged a skin which had about it a wholly inconsistent freshness. He saw me looking at him. I offered him a drink and he shifted over on the bench beside me. There was no doubt about it, his skin was like a boy's, and now that he was within a couple of feet of me, I could see another odd little thing: it was not only smooth and tanned like well-cared-for leather but it was covered with a peculiar down. I found myself wondering whether he could ever have shaved. But he interrupted my rather personal inventory. Perhaps he felt self-conscious at my look; perhaps he felt he ought to do something in exchange for the drink.

"You're interested in voyages?" he asked rather tentatively.

"I want to get the last of the whaling stories," I told him.

"Afraid I can't help you there. But," he hesitated, "you wouldn't be interested in polar exploration?"

I remarked that whaling led in that direction. He seemed to wish to talk—gave me the impression I'd be doing him a service by listening.

"You haven't done that?" I asked half-encouragingly.

Again he replied with a question. "Do you remember an expedition when one man had to drop out to give the others a chance to get through?"

"That's a common predicament," I was saying when a particular incident suddenly flashed through my mind.

"You're not. . . ?"

"Perhaps not; perhaps not." He was suddenly evasive.

"But when I've told you what I've been through, you won't care who I am and perhaps you'll even understand why I don't, either."

Suddenly he seemed to become alive. He glanced at me almost humorously.

"The Ancient Mariner only wanted to talk about his Albatross—well, I want to talk about a bird, but polar, physically, to an albatross."

To hurry him on I tried to pin him down. "Polar?" I asked.

"But not North," he answered.

"No, I guessed . . ."

Then he was off. "Antarctica—the only, the last, unexplored continent! The North got men first, and what did it give? Not a continent; simply more sea. Haven't we enough? Three-fifths of the earth's covered with sea."

"Well, Antarctica isn't any better!"

"It's land."

"Frozen land's no better than frozen sea?"

"True enough; that's the point. Still, I don't know if it was true. Perhaps it was a delirium. But if so, how'm I here? Well, that's your problem now. That's for you to answer. Here it is straight. You know, I just walked out. There was a blizzard on. It's good, of course, as deaths go. You just plug ahead; don't have to bother where you're going, and when you feel numb you settle down and Nature, subzero Nature, the master anesthetist, does the rest. Well, I bumbled and stumbled, crawled a bit and sank. I woke gradually. It wasn't painful, so I knew I was dead. Another thing made me sure. I was moving, heaving, with a queer pulsing jerk. That, I thought, that's the way you feel your last heartbeats, as though they were something outside you, because you're already more'n half out of your body. But, if so, those jerks ought to have gotten weaker. Instead, they grew stronger. I was being pulled along, with big, swinging jerks. I must be on a sled, I thought. It was then that I began to give up the death idea.

"There was only one alternative: Rescue. I tried to shift, but found myself fast. Finally, I worked a goggle so I could see through a slit in the wrappings, sideways. The blizzard had stopped. The stars were dazzlingly clear. You remember, it was just at the end of the season when we were lost; we got late on our schedule. I lay awhile, peering out, watching a large star hanging clearly above the edge of the plain over which we'd tramped all those days, and now I was pulsing along. I was just turning over and over in my mind: what the dickens could be the team that could pull the way I was being pulled? when suddenly I stopped dead from wondering about that and switched to asking Where? For that bright star had crept down, down toward the horizon.

"Don't you see? I knew my bearings that amount, you bet. I was lying on my right side. The star was setting. We weren't going North—we were going South! Again I felt I must be dead, or mad. Anyhow, I was frightened out of my acquiescence. I forced my head up a bit so my goggles could get a line ahead. What I saw kept my neck cricked till it nearly broke.

"Yes, I was strapped to a sled heaped over with some wrapping. It was certainly effective enough, for I felt no excessive cold, though it must have been as cold as Dante's Hell. What did send cold right through me, though, was my—my retinue.

Of course, the sled jerked because the team that drew it literally bounded ahead; the going was smooth enough, but the animals that pulled sprang ahead with such odd leaps that, if I'd been sitting up I'd have been thrown off backward.

"But, though the team was odd, the teamsters held my attention. There were four of them. They ran alongside the 'dogs.' They were stocky figures with short boots, a curious, tailed coat and—I suppose, because of the frightful cold—queer long-nosed masks. I could see the light of the quarter moon, which was low behind us, gleaming on their masks as they turned their heads a bit to and fro as they ran. They were so wrapped up that my alarm for myself was almost forgotten in my amazement at the speed at which they ran—they seemed almost to skim along the frozen ground with their thickly swathed arms held out a little from their bulky bodies.

"Still, I don't think your anthropological interest in the physical prowess of any kind of savage would have kept your mind off yourself if you'd looked, as I naturally did, a little farther ahead. There was no longer a possible shadow of doubt about it. We were bundling along as fast as any dog-team's ever scurried, I was tied up as neatly as a corpse and bound, not for rescue, home, and glory—no, bound for the ultimate cold storage—the absolute refrigeration. I hadn't been wrong about that star—no such luck. The view ahead left no doubt. We were climbing up a vast slope.

"I must say to my credit that I spared a moment from the misery of my predicament to admire the speed which my captors and their team kept up, breasting that slope. I might have been wrong about East and West—not about North and South. You know, Antarctica rises, sweeping up from the northern seacoast and the Great Ice Barrier to that awe-inspiring range from which tower those two most terrible peaks in the world—the volcanoes aptly named Erebus and Terror—infernal fire blasting out on infernal cold. Poor little life shudders away as these two ancient enemies rush out at each other.

"Well, there we were, swinging along up that slope to where those awful bastions of the Inferno towered above us. The most modest fancy that flitted through my pulsing head was that some mad, unknown Eskimo cannibals were whisking off this windfall of fresh meat to broil it in some convenient larva crack.

"I suppose I was terribly exhausted. I must have dozed off, because I had failed to keep my lookout. Anyhow, next time I squinted ahead we had made wonderful progress. The team was still bounding ahead, the flapping teamsters still prancing along beside them, and we were far up the slope at the top of which I felt sure my sorry miseries would end. That was true enough. But truth was stranger than my wildest dread. The jerking was extremely tiring in itself, and, of course, I was nearly dead with fatigue to start with. It doesn't matter whether you call it a dead faint or a sleep of complete exhaustion.

"My next waking did what I'd certainly have bet was impossible—it beat my first—and beat it hollow—so hollow that though I remembered my start at that first come-to, at that second I thought again that now at last it must be true—this *is* death—this kind of grim nonsense can only take place after death, after one has taken leave of the last vestiges of the world of common sense. It couldn't fit into this earth, anyhow, anywhere. This, baldly, is what I saw. I was still more or less on my back, so that's why I first noticed the sky. There wasn't a star in it. It was all fogged over. Nothing odd in that, you'll say. But wait a minute. It was all fog, but a fog such as I've never seen before or since. For a moment I thought my sight had gone, that, perhaps, in the afterlife everything was vague and misty. If I am alive, I reflected, I've lost the power to focus. It was—how shall I put it?—like looking up at the flies in the transformation scene of a pantomime, only all out of focus. There was wave upon wave of fringes, skirts, curtains, all of some filmy, faintly fluted draping. They rustled as they undulated. The sound was so quiet and natural that, since I couldn't see them clearly enough to judge their distance, I thought they must be near, perhaps twenty or thirty feet above my head.

"But, if the form was ambiguous, the color was—well, I have to work that word pretty hard—*amazing*. You know the colors of a large vacuum tube when current's in it? The whole of what I was looking up at was flushing and pulsing as it was washed by these tides of uncanny color.

"Perhaps it was the word 'pulsing' that made me realize that the actual pulsing had stopped. Yes, I was at a standstill or, rather, at a lie-still. Perhaps it was dumb to wish I could see what all those eerie searchlights were falling on. I tried to raise my head and at once felt a curious broad hand helping me. But what I saw made me forget the odd feel, forget the odd sky. Oh, I could see well enough. There was nothing wrong with my eyes. If anything was wrong, it was with my brain.

"I was still lying on the sled, and my goggles and wrappings were gone. But there was no need for them. It was warm, damply warm. And there was no doubt that I was still out of doors. Why that made me go back again to the belief that I was dead—gone for good from this world—I don't know, though neither of 'the other places' are said to be 'muggy,' are they?

"But I couldn't keep my mind on the climate, any more than on the lighting. For I wasn't alone. Standing close about me, looking down on me—but with their long-nosed masks still on, so that I couldn't judge their expression—were my captors, rescuers, kidnapers, what you will. I gazed at their snow kit with the dull amazement of a very small child looking for the first time at a diver in his inflated suit and valve-fitted helmet. And then my amazement turned to dismay—dismay, disgust, yes, horror. I was, you see, trying to make sense of these people—to pierce, as it were, their disguise: trying to judge, behind their masks, what their intentions were toward me. And then—it was as bad as seeing ghosts—I suddenly saw that they weren't disguised; they weren't wrapped up. They hadn't any clothes on, not a stitch! Then what did they have on?—these bulky, booted, masked fellows?

"I say again"—his voice cracked with a very convincing accent of dismay—"they had no clothes on, and yet, true enough, they were able—just as I saw them equipped then—to trot about in subzero cold.

"You've guessed? No, you couldn't. I know I struggled I

don't know how long against believing my eyes, for the light, though pulsing, was like a torrent of floodlighting. There was, I tell you, never a moment's doubt as to what I was seeing. The resistance came from my owning up to the clear meaning of what I saw. I struggled with all my might to believe that I was looking at masked kidnapers, inquisitors, anything you like, however dangerous and dreadful, as long as it was human. And all the time my eyes kept on saying to me—yes, and will you believe me?—the last, unnerving touch, my nose, too was saying it: What you are looking at—these things that are close enough for you to smell, are big, giant big, bigger than most men, but not men—they're big bipeds, big stalking birds! Yes, that was it. Under that insanely colored sky, as though in some grotesque, glass-lidded aviary, I lay, shrunken like Alice after she'd eaten the mushroom, looked down on by those large, powerful birds.

"I own, at that, my last vestiges of interest in topography fled. I remember recalling instead, and most infelicitously, Wells's grim story, *Aepyornis Island,* about the man who came within an ace of being pecked to death by his pet, a giant bird.

"And I was these creatures' captive. They swayed their heads a little. Their glassy eyes regarded me, but what I regarded was the way the glittering varicolored light ran up and down their long, strong, polished, pointed beaks. I don't know whether the next thing was a relief. It ought to have been. For at least it made clear that my immediate fear wasn't going to be practiced on me without delay. But the way I learned that was itself so shocking that I think I was more upset then than ever. I suppose we fear madness more than pain or death. And this forced me, I felt, one step nearer madness.

"These creatures weren't disguised men. I'd faced up to that shock—a nasty enough one, in all conscience. And then there was another one, right on—as one might say—the other side of the jaw of my reason. For this shock was just the reverse of the first. I couldn't resist the evidence of my ears as I'd tried to hold out against that of my eyes. These creatures, these birds, were talking to each other—talking about me. Of course, I couldn't understand a word. But when half-a-dozen stout old gentlemen, standing around a man on his back, look at him, point fat, flipperish hands at him, and then turn and quack at each other and then look at him and quack again—Well, then I say it's no use; the game's up: they are birds—which is bad enough—and they are discussing his disposal.

"Of course, you see what is coming, don't you? Why, after a few fell-considered—yes, I know they were—remarks, the senior and gravest of all the company turned to me again and requested—requested my co-operation. There couldn't be a doubt about that. Well, I did what you'd have done. I nodded, coughed, cleared my throat. And, believe me, after that exhibition of myself, of my superior human readiness and address, I felt I was the dumb bird. They weren't dumb by any means.

"Again they considered. Finally I felt that queer paw on my back and smelled that queer musky bird-smell, and then I was assisted to my feet. Of course, I felt extremely odd—odd beyond words. I think the air itself is odd there; through the bird-smell I could catch quite strong whiffs of sulphur and ozone also. Those people haven't any sense of smell; they have rather different senses from ours, but I'll get to that later. Of course, I was dead-beat, though they had already evidently given me some sort of cordial before I quite came to. There was a queer, keen taste in my mouth and throat. Anyhow, you wait till you find yourself strolling along, courteously assisted by two giant birds, who—metaphorically and actually, since they stood about seven feet high—are carrying on a conversation over your head. You see if you won't feel a bit giddy.

"Still, I noticed quite a few things. For instance, we were going along a path—not much of a path, but quite a well-beaten trail. You couldn't see far because just then the atmosphere was so iridescent. It wasn't what you'd call fog—though, as I've said, the temperature must have been over sixty and the humidity was high. It was the strange flickering light; as if the whole ill-defined sky were a sort of rainbow badly off color and quite unable to pull itself together into a decent arch with properly outlined bands.

"But interest in general meteorology was again brought back to earth with a bump. Right ahead of me loomed—houses. They weren't much as architecture. They appeared to be built of uncut stones piled together with no clear courses. But when I was close enough, I saw that the stones were all set in hard mortar and were well smoothed and fitted.

"When we reached the first of these huts, my companions wheeled around and gently ushered me inside the place. One stayed with me while the other disappeared. When he returned, he was holding a covered dish in his bill. There was a small table in the room, but no chair—nothing at all to sit on, or to lie on, for that matter. Just that small table, nothing else, though the bareness of the room's four walls was relieved by a kind of alcove in one place, a sort of doorless and shelfless cupboard. The creature which had come in with the dish placed it on the table and deftly whisked off the cover. It was a large soup plate full of what looked like a thick broth. My two guardians looked at me, bowed with an odd mixture of the ridiculous and the stately, and marched out. I was hungry; the broth smelled good. It tasted better. It was also very filling. As there was nowhere to sit and nowhere to go, after eating the broth, I lay on the floor and fell asleep. I'd become used to sleeping on the ground—you know, half over on your face, your hands curled around your head.

"I don't know how long I slept. I woke to find the light the same, quivering but just as bright, and, of course, my watch was long dead. Looking up, I found a 'guardian' looking at me with that expressionless attention which these creatures had. I scrambled to my feet, and he bowed low to the doorless doorway—the window had no glazing or frame, either. I was quite ready to see all I could; I felt refreshed and was more curious than anxious now. But he led me away from—what shall I call it?—the Penguinry? We followed a path which led straight towards a steep cliff, the top of which was lost in the iridescent mist. When we reached the cliff, we saw a cleft in it. This turned out to be the opening of a very narrow canyon, its walls not more than some six feet apart and going up pretty sheer till along the top one could see a ribbon of pulsing light—the sky, as it appeared in that odd place. Our path, which was smooth sand—the bed of some stream that once had issued through this cleft, I suppose—opened into a small amphitheater—after perhaps five or six loops and bends. The place was small, but up till then it was the most wonderful spot I'd ever seen.

"Talk of the Forty Thieves' cave in *Ali Baba!* All the rocks were of different colors; but that's simply to start with. The amazing thing was that they all seemed to be lit from within. They were partly translucent and were partly glowing with a queer radiance that seemed to flush out from their crystalline structure. Then I realized what, of course, it must be: They were fluorescing. The queer sky above must, for some reason, have been making these queer minerals—just as labradorite and other such do—send back a kind of light-echo, a sort of secondary radiation. But there nearly every rock seemed to have its own flush and pulse of color. You've never seen color until you've seen stuff like this. And that wasn't the end of the show which was being put on for me to gape at.

Out of these glowing rocks with their iridescent bloom and glow, and over them, flowed streams of steaming water in colors, waters like champagne, like burgundy, like chartreuse—purple, gold, amethyst. These cascades formed in fonts and pools; they tumbled over weirs which heaped up foam of every color and tint. The rivulets flowed off musically into culverts and grottoes, in the dusk of which they shone with a glowing phosphorescence.

"The floor of this domeless cave of wonder was a sand that sparkled like gold and diamond dust. Yet there was nothing harsh or garish about any of this close-packed splendor. The entire area was literally bathed in an opalescent mist.

From the waters rose wreaths of steam across which shimmered half-formed rainbows.

"I turned to my guide. All he did was to wave a flipper toward the bubbling terraces; then he turned about, stalked off, and vanished around the first turn of the canyon cleft. My wish and what I took to be his intention chimed. I was out of my clothes and into one of those pools almost before his stiff tail feathers had whisked around the corner of a coral rock. I can't say I've ever bathed before or since. In comparison with that"—he sought for a poetic word in which to cloak his bare and timid emotion—"that laving—why one can only wallow, out here. The quality of that water! It tingled; tiny bubbles pricked your skin; it was like being combed, massaged, relaxed, stimulated, buoyed and plunged, needle-sprayed and warm-packed all at once. I shouted for sheer physical joy, and the strange polished rocks through the rush of the waters, gave back strange harmonics of my call. Out of pure animal spirits I threshed the foaming water and with my hand struck the glass-smooth sides of the pool in which I lay. A huge stalactite rose from the pool's lip, depending from and seeming to support an absurdly fretted gothic canopy overhead. I hit the smooth shaft with my palm. A beautiful deep note, as of a great bell, sounded through the place.

"I laughed like a child at the lovely joke of it all. Then, through my modest pink curtains of mist, I caught sight of my guide peeping discreetly around the edge of the rose-red cleft behind which he had retired—like an insect concealing itself in the petals of a tropical flower. I felt gayer, more trustful, more adventurous than I've felt since I was three and my nurse was giving me my bath.

"'I'm coming,' I shouted, quite certain in a way that this was all a Christmas Night dream after seeing the pantomime and getting home and looking over my presents and playing with the new rubber duck in the bath, and so to bed with nurse having just tucked me in.

"I skipped out of my font and felt so light that my sense of being out of my body was quite convincing. I felt clothed in a new kind of vitality. My skin and flesh seemed glowing and supple and all of it as strong as muscle. I felt as though I, too, must be glowing, fluorescing, pouring out the vitality with which that fountain of youth had charged me. I looked down at my body. I could have believed that I was lit by an eternal fire. Then I saw, lying on that dazzling sand, one stain—the wretched clouts in which I had been wrapped and must now wrap up again. I put on my wretched, stiff, soiled togs but their greasy stiffness was revolting to my skin, which seemed to have a new sense of touch. As I crossed the arena floor my guide peeped out again. If he hadn't, I don't know if I could have found my way out of the place. The fluted walls concealed the entrance so effectively that it seemed as though the rocks had closed behind the entrant, as in the Ali Baba cave. Every yard of the place's sheer sides was fretted and molded.

"He trotted ahead of me, leading me back to my hut and, bowing me in, stood with his back to me, blocking the door and looking out into the street. Again, I gathered, this was his tact. For now, lying on the table where the soup bowl had been, was an odd-looking object. On picking it up I discovered it was a cloak, beautifully light in weight, more delicate than silk to the touch, smelling of musk, pale gray in color, and woven in some strange way out of small feathers. I have never worn any kind of garment which seemed less like something one puts on and more like something that grows as naturally as one's hair out of one's skin. The contrast of the change, from my coarse stiff wrappings that were fettering my cleansed body into this cloak, gave me a feeling almost as delicious as I had when I had first plunged into the rock pool. I'd hardly thrown the robe around myself before the guide twirled about, then made that sweep with his head and stumped off ahead of me.

"One thing, at least, was now clear: I wasn't being treated as a captive. Indeed, so great was this—this people's courtesy that I wasn't even being treated as a curiosity—though I could imagine the kind of attention a huge, misshapen, feathered man would arouse if led on foot through the main street of one of our hamlets. As I went down the street I saw plenty of these strange beings about, but none—save an occasional chick or two—even turned its head as I passed. Of course, whether their features showed surprise or humor I couldn't then judge. A bird's bill is just the most pointed opposite of what novelists call their heroine's lips—tremulous, liquid and all that.

"I didn't, however, then have much time to think over this. For within a few hundred yards I'd been brought to a hut twice the size of any of the others, which ended this small street or lane. It had two steps in front of it and a high doorway, but again no door. We passed over the threshold, and, in the dusk within, I saw that a sort of court was sitting. My guide waited just inside the threshold, and so, of course, did I. Six creatures were drawn up along one side and six on the other; and, at the end, on a slightly raised platform facing us, the chairman, or chairbird was standing. One of the six on my left had been standing forward, quacking to the rest, but directing his remarks to the chair. As we entered, he drew back into line, and the chairman apparently answered him. Then, after a pause, the 'chair' must have said something that closed the proceedings, for the six brace, pair by pair, walked out, three on each side of us, and we were left facing the president.

"He quacked again, and my guide bowing to him and then to me, waved me forward. At that, my guide turned away, the chairman came down off his one-step dais, and I was directed to a small doorway in the side wall. These people are austere, I thought; they don't allow any sitting, even at public business. But when I entered the room off the Council Chamber I realized, as by then I suppose I ought to have guessed, that the absence of chairs in the public rooms and in the others was not a hardship or a discourtesy. This—this species never sat except when hatching eggs. That alcove in the room I was given—I found that every house had one. It was a sort of 'sentry box' affair. In it these creatures would stand, slightly inclined, while they slept. That was the only kind of resting place they required.

"In spite of the fact that I saw they always meant to be considerate, I thought this interview was going to be a little embarrassing, for, even with the best will in the world, how were we to get on? Yet, believe me, there wasn't a hitch from the start.

"As soon as we were closeted together, the chairbird bowed again and beckoned me to one of the window sills—the room had two windows opposite each other. He indicated that he wished me to be seated; evidently he had tumbled to the fact that I belonged to a species that didn't find it comfortable never to be off its feet. As soon as he saw me settled he caught my eye. Then, with a sweep of his flipper, or perhaps I'd better be anthropomorphic and say his hand—for it was a hand with three very stout but, as I soon learned, deft, fingers —he pointed to a bowl of water which was standing on the sill of the window opposite. As he did so, he looked quickly at me with his head turned to one side. Somehow, the gesture was quite unmistakable. 'Bowl,' I said. He listened for perhaps a couple of seconds and then, as clear as a Congo gray parrot, he said ringingly, 'Bowl,' and pointed to the water in it. 'Water,' I called. With scarcely a second's pause he echoed 'Water,' with just my inflection.

"We had a hour or more of this, as quick as that. We ran over every kind of object he could point to: the stones the room was walled and floored with—my eyes, teeth, hair; his feathers, bill, and feet. He seemed never to forget a word and hardly ever asked me to repeat one. And, would you believe it, at the close of our interchange, he made up some quite good sentences, ending with, 'We two here when you second time rested.' I felt that a linguist having that sort of power was quite right in wasting no time in trying to teach me 'the language of the birds.' After he had spoken his farewell sentence, he relaxed from the somewhat bent attention with which, to make certain of hearing the sounds I made, he had craned forward his seven-foot stature. He resumed his stately stance, emitted a kind of soft whistle—and there was my guide looking discreetly around the doorway.

We all bowed to one another again and off I went, led back to my room, to my supper—this time some kind of queer but delicately flavored fruits with a slight tang of resin. Queer, having desert fruit at the South Pole. And when I looked at them closely it was perhaps even queerer to realize that, as far as I could judge, they didn't belong to any genus of plant I'd ever seen. I remember thinking that, after all, since this was a continent more on its own than even Australia or New Zealand, it would have quite different sorts of plant life. But, then, how the mischief could they have developed themselves here! Well, it was clear there were so many problems here that if I were to try to solve them without more information, I should just worry myself blue.

"I was among friends, if friendship meant taking care not only of one's wants but of one's feelings as well. The supper of fruit was not only varied and very palatable, but, so quick were my hosts to realize my human limitations, that I found a bed in the corner of the room—or should I call it a nest? It had been made for me from a number of cloaks such as the one they had given me to wear.

"The next day my drill was repeated—that wonderful wash, then breakfast, and once more to the courthouse. The first hour was hardly over before the chairbird was doing almost as much talking as I. He made me understand what their actions certainly suggested, that I was welcome. He told me—how he did it with the still scanty vocabulary that he commanded was almost as much a wonder as the fact that already he used, with scarcely an error or a slip of forgetfulness, several thousand words, I reckon—that an expedition—which was a rare event with them—had been out in the farther world. I began to blush, I admit, when I tumbled to the fact that what he was trying to tell me was that he and his people had been watching our expedition with some trepidation (we, of course, had had no idea that we were being observed). They had felt that we were a possible peril, but after they had seen one of the party ready to go out to his death in order that the others might have a chance to survive, they had concluded that any creature which could behave in that way should not only be succored—regardless of any possible danger to the rescuers—but that such a creature might understand their way of life and give them useful sidelights on it.

"That fact was all that seemed to interest him. Why we were exploring and where we came from did not seem to excite his curiosity in the slightest. What seemed his wish was that I should understand something about them. He remarked that if I would be so good, he would like to practice human speech with me until he became tolerably proficient in it. 'There is much which we need to see through other eyes than ours,' he said, 'and that will take time and many new words.' It did take 'many new words,' but far less time than I would have supposed. Every day our 'lesson' brought us to further mastery of human speech, and soon he was as much at home in abstract terms as he was in concrete words; indeed, more at home than I myself was. Certainly, that bird had a master mind and evidently had thought very clearly in his own tongue about subjects which were, most of them, just on the fringe of my thoughts. Time and again I just didn't know the words for some thought he wanted to express in English. So you can imagine what happened. We built up a sort of pidgin—or, I should say, Penguin—English, 'Basic English' for birds. I'm sure if I could remember some of his clever phrases and coined words, you'd see how apt they were.

"One of the first things he explained to me—really as a kind of exercise for himself, to see if he could talk freely about subjects that needed a lot of rare words and abstract terms—was why they had given me these grand baths. Of course, I'd seen that his bird-people didn't wash, didn't need to. They had a wonderful preening drill, and, after that, their plumage was as glossy as if it had been varnished. 'Your bath,' he explained, 'was something in the nature of an experiment. We felt—for reasons which I will explain more fully when you possess more facts and I more words—that you might be incommoded by this peculiar climate unless we could do something to give you a kind of cover which you lacked, something to take the place of our plumage. We had, of course, known for some time that these radioactive springs, in which we wanted you to bathe, did have a remarkably beneficial effect on the skin of thinly coated non-birds. We find that they enable the skin to tolerate—and even benefit from—the ultraviolet light of this sky. Indeed, if I may say so, you have already benefited from the treatment.'

"He was right. My skin had been in pretty poor shape after our hardships, and, with a sudden rush or flush, if I may so say, had taken on a new kind of smooth suppleness. Indeed, I believe I've never quite lost the good effects of that treatment. All the time I was there I felt extraordinarily well; blood and skin seemed to glow. Later I understood how necessary this was: not merely to make me feel fit, but to screen me from danger which I did not suspect. I don't know how long it took—maybe it was a fortnight, I don't think it was more—before this fine old creature felt that he had enough command of my language to launch into a discussion with me of general topics, or, what he called the explanation that I required.

"We had met for our morning session and, as he liked me to begin, I started that day by saying that the place was rather a surprise. I considered that a courteous understatement. His only reply was a question: 'And ourselves even more so?' By the way, I'd learned by that time how to recognize the way humor could be shown in their otherwise expressionless faces. They would flicker that third eyelid which birds have in the corner of their eyes. This was a kind of solemn wink they gave when they were joking.

"I allowed that, perhaps, I had been a bit surprised by that, too. My surprise, of course, had been acute to the point of alarm; but I believe that that old bird, though he didn't ever frighten me, did surprise me more than anything I'd seen or heard before in that unbelievably odd place. Certainly his next remark gave no quarter to my self assurance. I had told him, as a sort of introduction to some questions on my part, that we humans had had a great imaginative writer who had hated mankind—with good reason—and therefore had written a story about an imaginary place where men were beasts and horses were supermen. My companion asked me a little about horses—what sort of animal they were and what their relationship was with us.

"For a moment he thought over what I had told him and

then he remarked, 'Then they are really of the same stock as yourselves, warm-blooded and mammals, but creatures which have lost their hands?' I was surprised, need I say, that this bird knew about evolution, but simply confirmed his remark by telling him about the descent of the horse from a small five-toed animal. He reflected a moment more and then added, 'That was a mistake of your storyteller. Of course, it is clear that a horse would have to be, must now be, a stupid animal, even if kind. No, if your imagineer had had real insight he would have chosen, for his example, a bird.' I thought this was pretty vain but, of course, quite natural—every creature thinks it is the highest type. He guessed my thought. 'I know that sounds to you a typical bird fancy. Being a bird, of course I think we are the form in which Life is best expressed. So perhaps you will excuse me if I make my case an aviary apology!' His third eyelid slid, a gray shadow for a moment, over his bright, steady eye, and then he continued:

"'After I have told you the story, I believe that you will agree with me that the history of our great order, the order of birds, proves my thesis. You know, I see, the main outline. There are only two great divisions of life, you and ourselves: both came up from the cold-blooded stupidity of the lizards; we are the only two alternative ways of answering Life's question. 'Would you know more, would you not only live but understand, not only enjoy but also create?' But, if you will forgive me, we are the more vital, the more energetic. We probably started out on the path of continuous consciousness—that continuous consciousness that warm blood compels—long before your first mammal ancestor, the tree shrew, acquired the power. Yet I must confess that, long before you could waste your talent for progress, we wasted ours. You have wanted to be able to move with real freedom, to be able to fly. One of your small mouse cousins—we have a species here—does it not uncreditably—though not very graciously; and some of the squirrel lot can slide a little on the air. But you, the leaders of the mammal line, you can't fly at all. You have danced, and, forgive me if I note, looking at your physique, that such dancing must be very clumsy. Beside the turn of a fish in water—let alone the sweep of a bird on the wing—you are creatures caught in their own egg membrane, if I may so put it, all ligatured and bound. At last, you now fly, in a way, I understand, but more like a flying fox and, alas; not as we did—though we did it in an unwise exultation—for fun.'

"Since he seemed so imperturbable, I thought I would answer then.

"Your frame," I remarked, "doesn't look even as suitable as ours for dancing or flying."

" 'That is an essential part of my story,' he replied, going on evenly. 'As I was saying, millions of years ago nearly all the birds, out of sheer joy of living, leaped into the air. They could no longer wait or endure the plodding ways of life on the earth. They gave up the patient fingering of things in order to swim free in the greater ocean of the sky. They hankered for the lovely lazy freedom of the sea, the perfection of rhythmic movement, and they spent the gift of their new high energy in recapturing that bodily rapture that seemed lost forever when life crawled out onto the muddy, dusty, rough, and heavy land. They treated the land simply as a bridge they could cross, a bridge from which they might spring from a lesser freedom to a greater.

" 'Of course, it was a mistake, an attempt to win a freedom which, at that level, could only be an irresponsibility—a wish to hurry on to new experiences before the earlier, slower, harder ones had been mastered. But not all the birds made this mistake. Not all. We penguins, in particular, abstained from that headlong flight—that escape from close-up understanding. Some birds, as you probably know, first flew and then forgot how to fly. They had sold their hands for wings and then never recovered what they had sold; they made the worst of both worlds—they could neither enjoy nor create. But we, the penguins, never flew. We avoided that oubliette into the void.'

"His third eyelid flickered over his eye. I smiled in reply. I was perched, as usual, in the window ledge, and he was perambulating majestically up and down the floor, quacking this astounding story—this alternative to what we, in our pride, have taken to be the one track of evolution.

" 'Well," he ruminated, 'I think I may say the penguins, on the whole, haven't been bad fellows. We were no worse a stock from which to start the final climb to the summit of understanding than the base from which your lot made their sortie—the small apes, and, back of them, the tree shrews. Our lot were kindly, social, fond of fun, and, though yours may have had more native curiosity, perhaps we were more largely endowed with the sympathy which is the understanding of the heart and—' He paused, and I thought that through his bill came a sound resembling a human sigh— 'and which exacts as high a price as does any other form of exploration and daring trust. You know that when the first white men found our poor cousins on the seashore of this continent, our cousins, taking these men to be rather unshapely second cousins—for we have the belief in our bones that friendship is the sense of life—went up to the visitors and, since we build our homes of stones, offered the newcomers a few good pebbles to help them in housebuilding; and we bowed, to indicate that they were welcome and would have our help if they needed it.' He paused, and I thought I saw his bill going a little higher into the air. 'The men seized our defenseless cousins and threw them—alive—into boiling water in order to wring a little oil from their poor bodies.'

"I confess I was looking at the floor when he finished his sentence. I had heard the story before but, coming from the mouth of an imperial penguin—well, I went more pink with shame for my species than I'd been when I came out of that first bath. Seeing my confusion, he went quickly on. 'As I've said, the stock was not without promise, for, indeed, these poor people of the coast are somewhat decadent; the stock they and we spring from was brighter than they are now, or have been for long. Anyhow, one day a group of us, under some pressure of events about which I am still uncertain—perhaps the arrival of mammals such as the bear—decided to move; to leave the coast and strike into the unknown. I think it must have been some intrusion that made us move, for we claim—at least our women do—' again his eye flickered, 'that we, the oldest of the birds, were actually on this continent when, as its flora still shows and its coal measures bear witness, it was part of the primal continent near the equator. The women, then, claim that everyone else is an alien.

" 'The fact is, we did decide to move, to go south. Cold is a great friend. The greatest plenty of life in the sea crowds up near the ice. The greatest animals the world has ever seen, the giant whales, choose to live there, too. Life likes stimulant.'

"I looked out at the warm mugginess and he took in my glance and read it.

" 'When you have gone through the ice, then you may come to open water again; when you have been through the glacial age, then you may rest, for you have won. It was a bold trek, that, to leave the coast and the good fishing and to seek an unpromised land where the land itself seems to be rising until it touches the icy sky, and, where it touches, the volcanoes pour out flame. But it was just that, as you will see, that gave us quite half our natural capital. Well, the waddling ancestors came over the pass across which you have been towed lately, and found their destiny.'

"He bowed. 'Now you must be tired. Tomorrow I will be able to explain better. As my words are still few and ill-chosen, it will be easier for you to understand what I have yet to tell you if we walk around the place. There you will see actual illustrations of what I would like to describe.'

"I need hardly tell you that I was ready to be taken to the presence as soon as he was prepared for me the following day. As soon as I had joined him, he strode out, I trotting alongside him like a small child beside a very big and bulky nurse. As we went down the little street, the people bowed to him, and he placed his hand on his breast at every salutation.

"'What you have seen,' he remarked, looking sideways and down at me as we went along, 'is but a corner of our small but rich heritage.' We had left the village behind and, instead of taking the way toward the bathing canyon, we skirted the precipices concealing it. 'This,' he began again, 'is perhaps the best time of year to see the whole place. I should explain to you why.' That queer childish hymn came into my mind, 'There is no night in Heaven.' I asked, 'Is it never dark here?'

"'Hardly ever,' he replied, 'though the volume of light alters considerably.'

"'Do you never see the clear sky?'

"'Very seldom, and then not so clearly as you can on a fine night or day, outside.'

"'That's rather a disadvantage,' I rejoined unreflectively.

"'On the contrary,' he took me up. 'Except for that we should be incapable of living here. But, for a moment, look at the view.'

"He had strolled up to where a long slope now touched the foot of a remarkable precipice. As we turned around, with our backs to it, the view that met us was, I have no doubt, quite the finest I have ever seen, or ever shall see. Nowhere in the rest of the world, I believe, could there be such an arresting landscape. It wasn't large but it was quite large enough. The sky had lifted a bit, and the lighting was more settled, less pulsing, and of a more uniform tone. It was quite clear that one was looking at a huge crater, a crater as big as the one near the great African lakes or the full-sized ones in the moon, a crater in which a county might be sunk quite comfortably. The crater wall ran around in a series of magnificent precipices, mostly cloud-capped. For a tide of white fog kept surging over them and on the lip one saw numerous cataracts, while plumes of white smoke trailed up above the columns of spray. I have never seen what is called inanimate nature so vividly animated.

" 'You see, of course,' said his Highness, 'that the peculiar effect we have here is due to the coming together of a number of rare factors. This place is still very active volcanically. The ground is warm in many places and, as you felt in the pool in which we thought it might do you good to bathe, many warm mineral springs break out.' We gazed round the huge hollow. It was clear that the well-known richness of volcanic soil was having its effect. Long groves of trees, hung thickly with vines, gave the place an almost tropical look. And as we gazed downward at the heart of these groves, I could see a considerable expanse of water.

" 'That is the central crater lake,' the Penguin remarked to me. 'All the waters drain into it. We have never sounded it. Where they go to, no one knows.'

" 'Why don't you sound it?' I asked casually.

" 'Because we are interested in other explorations.'

" 'What?' I went on asking, 'what other explorations?' I had gathered they were uninterested in the rest of the world.

" 'I think that first you should see all there is to see before hearing all we can tell you.' It wasn't a rebuff; it was only a direction.

" 'First I think I ought to tell you,' he continued, 'a little about our climate. A moment ago I said that this was the best time of year to see the place. You may have discovered for yourself why that is so. The sun has just now left us to the polar night. When the sun's rays are exercised on our atmosphere they clear it. This, of course, is a commonplace of radioactivity. The extraordinary lighting you have noticed is due to the cosmic radiation causing these auroras which are so intense at midwinter that the light then is brighter, though more confused, than when the sun is over the horizon. Just when the sun is arriving and when it is departing or just gone, there is a kind of balance between its light and this electrical illumination and then, as I have said, our visibility is at its best and the beautiful but confusing lighting caused by fluorescence is less. In the polar night we are not in darkness, you see, but, as it were, in a kind of rainbow dreamland of light. This has many consequences which I will go into later. At present I only want to point out how fortunate it is that you are here at this time. It allows you to have a better view of our territory, and there are also other even more important advantages, which you will understand better when I can explain more.'

"We spent that day and the next couple of weeks making expeditions over the whole place. I saw the pass through which I had been brought, and we went down to the shore of the central lake, the very floor of the crater. There the air was distinctly heavier than on the level where the villages lay. For the one in which I stayed, though the place of residence of 'the government,' was, like a score of others, built on the same contour. Few of these people lived near the lake itself, though the spot was perhaps the most beautiful of all the lovely places in that sunken country. The water was generally of a quality of violet I never remember seeing anywhere else. There must have been some chemicals in solution in it. And, as the variegated sky changed through the hues of the spectrum, the lake glowed like a peacock's neck. A number of small rivers wound their ways quietly through deep meadows and fed this still water.

" 'I think I could stay here for good,' I remarked one day when the king penguin and I returned from a survey that now had given me a pretty comprehensive idea of the place.

" 'We have naturally considered that that might be your wish,' he replied with his usual quiet manner of anticipating my thought. 'But before you could think of that you would have to know a great deal more about this place. I suppose there is no place in the world where so much seems to be presented and, in actual fact, so little is given away.' The third eyelid flickered several times before he resumed. 'You see, though you have seen what I grant is a wonderful appearance, you have, in point of fact, not the slightest idea of what is behind all this.'

"I thought he was going to give me a lecture on the simple life, good, free government, and the general need of being less human and more birdlike. But I was mistaken. He meant, as he always did, precisely what he said. That place was odd, odder than it was lovely, and that is saying as much as one can. His next remark, though a question, was a bit uncanny.

" 'Have you ever heard of arctic hysteria?'

"I said I had heard that living north of the arctic circle even the toughest men might become odd and excitable, and might even see and hear things that weren't there. 'Yes,' said the wise old bird, 'it's true. No doubt, we are very considerably acclimatized and yet, even we have to take care.'

"Then, seeming to change the subject, he asked another question: 'Are you interested in mutations?'

"Again I was able to say that I supposed I knew as much as the next field naturalist about the things that hadn't been discovered about the important problems of breeding. This led to a third question:

" 'Have you studied cosmic radiation?'

"There, at last, I was able to give a flat 'no.' Then he did allow himself to do a bit of linking up:

" 'All three are very close to each other and I may say that there lies our main interest.'

"Of course, all this from a bird was still rather a shock to me, but—save for human high-brow moments like that—I was already getting to think that behind that massive bill and baldly staring bird's eyes there was a man's mind looking out at me; indeed, I might say a mind certainly better than most men's.

" 'Take the cosmic radiation first,' he remarked in his quiet, slightly quacking lecturer's voice. 'You have gathered, of course, that we are right on the South Pole. As I remarked to you some while ago when congratulating you on arriving when the visibility conditions are so good, what you see, and see through, is the aurora australis, the cosmic radiation which pours in at either pole and which, after three or four collisions, at last hits things slowly enough for us to see the luminous echoes, these southern lights. I am sure now that it is this radiation that causes polar hysteria. The tremendous electrical charge, as one would expect, upsets a nervous system not used to being exposed to it. Indeed, I am now sure that we ourselves, though acclimatized to the place, couldn't live here with this radiation if it were not for the fact that the volcanic heat throws up that cover of cloud or mist. In it, the radiation is screened. So we get a constant illumination and are safe from the invisible rays. I feel sure that a clear sky could not sufficiently screen out the deadly short rays.'

" 'But what's that got to do with mutations?' I said. I had noticed that the flora was very odd. As far as I could remember, I hadn't seen a bush or a shrub or any grass that I could identify, though some looked like queer derivatives of forms with which we are familiar.

" 'Everything,' was his reply. 'Literally, it accounts for everything; for the way we live; for the reason we are undisturbed; for the simplicity of our way of life, which, grant me, you find a little homely?'

"Perhaps rather unnecessarily I said, 'You must explain.'

"Again came a question: 'Did you notice the animals which drew your sled?'

"I remarked that I had seen them ahead of me in a poor light but when I was up and about they had been led away.

" 'Well, to be brief—for you don't need more than the outline to form a general opinion—our principal interest has been in the problems and possibilities of directed breeding. As you'd probably suspect if you thought it over, this place has a very high mutation rate because every living thing is being bombarded with rays that strike right at the nucleus of the chromosomes, right at the genes. As a consequence, we suffered for ages from the appearance of freaks—wild mutational sports. This was not particularly dangerous to us, however, since our oily feathers give us much protection, and when the egg is hatching, its shell, being of lime, protects it. And even then, the egg is always fully covered by one of the parents. But with plants and other animals it was very confusing.'

"I remarked that I had noticed a number of plants that seemed very odd to me. 'And not merely plants,' he remarked. Pushing aside some grass with his foot, he seemed to be watching the ground with that extraordinary concentration peculiar to birds. Suddenly he pounced on something with his beak. When he turned to me, he was holding in it, with delicate care, a small lizard. Then, rapidly slipping the small animal between two of his fingers and holding it close to me, he remarked, 'Do you notice anything odd about this little creature's scales? Look particularly down toward the tail.' I scanned it with care. 'Some of the scales have curious fringed ends,' I replied.

" 'That's it,' he remarked, with vivid interest. 'You see the significance? It is, of course, of great interest to us. For here, you see, is a lizard, beginning—as we believe *we* began millions of years ago—to transmute scales into feathers. This little creature is an actual mutation. If it doesn't knock up against some canceling mutation, I shouldn't be surprised if it turns into some creature like the Archaeopteryx—the first feathered lizard—and so give rise to a whole new family of birds. It was because we were always coming across things like this,' he said, gently putting the small creature on the grass again and letting it run away, 'that we decided to learn about mutation and radiation. That's our great—our predominant, interest now. Indeed, I think we may now say that we have at last succeeded in making the great tempest that spins through Space crack some of the nuts of knowledge for us. First, naturally we experimented with plants. We found out how and when to expose them to the sky: the proper time of the year—as the radiation fluctuates—and how far up in the altitude range. I think it's quite likely we should never have gotten as far as we have had we not also discovered that some of the rocks here are highly radioactive in themselves. It was this discovery, I believe, that was decisive. It allowed us, in the end to balance one charge against another, as it were. In consequence, we can now produce what we might, I believe, call results of precision. That's why I asked you if you had noticed the sled animals. They are some of our products. In a word what has become our absorbing aim is to see whether we can untie some of the knots into which evolution has wound itself. As you know, all animal and plant life is inevitably becoming more and more specialized, and eventually, if things are not unraveled, there will be no further possibility of originality or freedom left to any species. Even if they do not become extinct because of their powerlessness to respond creatively to their environment, they will become living fossils, incapable of enjoying any enterprise, liberty, or creativeness. What we then do is to regeneralize the creature which has become specialized. Those animals which drew you—well, come along and see the kennels.'

"He had been leading me up a slope, and I saw, in front of me, lines of low hutches. Then he gave his low penetrating whistle and out of the small doors, bounding and dancing on their hind legs, came some of the most live and active creatures I had ever seen.

" 'They were seals once,' he remarked, 'but, you see, they are now regeneralized.'

"And they were! Here was something which beat H. G. Wells's 'Dr. Moreau' all hollow. The front flipper had become, or perhaps I ought to say, had gone back to being, a kind of broad powerful hand enabling the creatures to bound along in the way that made the progress of the sled so swift and so pulsing. Their carriage and gait were similar to powerful large-headed kangaroos.' They stood up with their hands on his shoulders, their bright eyes darting all over the place and a strange variety of cheerful noises coming from their mouths.

" 'I know what they mean,' he remarked. 'In another generation or so, if we don't stabilize the experiment at the present point, they'll be speaking. On the whole, though, I think they'll be happier as creatures mainly of emotion and action rather than of thought and organization. Even when you give freedom, one freedom means that you must deny yourself another. In a society such as ours, tied by a true co-operation, perhaps it is better that some should have the utmost freedom of thought and others an equal and compensatory freedom of feeling. You see, as seals, they had in them, a very strong endowment of kinesthetic apprehension. In them life probably expresses itself most fully in movement.'

"He said something to them, and they raced away back to their homes. Then, turning to me, 'You see, this is why we don't need machines and never again shall. For what are machines but clumsy, stiff, artificial hands put upon our hands—just as a mutilated creature might be given an artificial limb. But if you can grow whatever you want, why toil to make it of clumsy, dead material? That's our goal—to win back the freedom that we, the warm-blooded creatures, lost when we emerged from the reptile stage. We can already make quite good replacements of the lost parts of limbs. I see, too, that you've noticed we have recovered our fingers. That was one of our first distinct triumphs.'

"He stated his proposition very quietly, and the example he had given me in these charming seal creatures was certainly not alarming. Yet when I thought it over, a hundred odd questions came surging into my mind. My first effort to state my puzzlement was, perhaps, a little crude. 'Do you really know what you're up to?' I asked him. 'I mean, have you really found out what life wants to do and how to bring it to its goal?'

"He didn't seem to be surprised at my question; on the contrary, I think he was rather pleased. What he said was:

" 'Well, now you'll find a visit to the hospital quite interesting, I believe. I think tomorrow we'll spend the morning in the hospital and then in the afternoon you'll be able to appreciate the laboratory all the more; as you might expect, they are adjoining.'

"The next day we took a trail that led us to the other side of the crater. Not long after we had passed the lake, I saw a series of buildings on a spur. After a few more hundred yards of walking, it was clear this was not a village but a series of special houses. We were greeted at the door by the creature who evidently had this whole department in its care. My guide and he exchanged some remarks, and, throwing open a door, he took us into a ward.

" 'This is Ward Number One,' said my instructor. 'It is the accident ward.'

"As I looked down the row of couches, I saw that not only were they occupied by those bird creatures, but that there were also some couches on which lay the seal creatures and several other forms of animals I had not seen before.

" 'We are carrying out repairs here,' he said, turning to me. 'Would you step over here and look at this case?' With his hand, he raised the paw of one of the seal creatures. 'It was crushed very badly,' he explained, 'under a stone. It was not a case of just healing a serious lesion, but of making the whole hand-pattern repeat itself—as it does in the womb.'

"I looked down at the hand, and, true enough, through the broken tissue it was clear that certain growing edges were beginning—I can use no other word—to sprout.

" 'If you will step over here,' he said, 'you'll see the same process of repair advanced about two weeks.' He held up a hand on which curious, dwarf fingers were appearing and the old, broken tissue was withering away as though it were dead skin of a blister. 'Of course, once we have the right stimulant to set the full repair process going, accident restoration is the simplest of all our work.'

"By this time we had reached the end of the ward, and his hospital superintendent had thrown open the door of what I suppose should be called the small operating theater. A patient was on the table and, through various filters and from various tubes, an injured limb was being radiated.

" 'Most of the light,' he said, 'is brought through certain

filters direct from the sky and, of course, to balance it, we have in these other tubes wave lengths of other intensities derived from the radioactive rocks. Here, I think we may say, we have instruments of such delicacy that we can really touch the mainspring and the minute but powerful generators of life itself.'

"The next door opened into another ward.

" 'These,' said my companion, 'are more interesting; biological problems. These are not accident cases. Here we are attempting to unravel the mystery of disease.'

" 'Most of them,' I remarked, 'look old.'

" 'Yes,' he remarked, 'you're right. You see, ill health hardly becomes a problem for us until a certain age. If anyone feels or shows impairment of vitality we soon can diagnose it. Just step across here, and I'll explain that.'

"His lieutenant, who seemed to follow his thought exactly, had already opened a small door inside the wall of the ward. It led to a room rather smaller than the operating theater.

" 'Would you mind,' my guide said, 'standing on that small square there?'

"I found that I was facing a panel in the wall that looked like black glass. He shut the door, and we were in total darkness. Then I heard a switch snap. The panel I was facing began to glow. It increased in brilliancy, and very rapidly I saw outlined on it a shadowy iridescent figure that seemed composed of layers of varicolored light. I heard my guide's voice at my shoulder.

" 'Of course, I am completely ignorant of the charges that compose your species. But just making a guess, because we are both warm-blooded creatures, I should surmise that your vitality is now fairly good. Moreover, I am pretty sure, from the way some of those fringes'—and I saw the shadow of his big finger indicating where certain bright lines seemed thrusting their way into less bright zones on the lit panel—'are growing, that any vitality you may have lost is now being rapidly restored. It is here that we check up on the health of our community, and by this method we can often tell when there is too much expenditure of energy, and then we can warn the patient to balance his life better.' He threw open the door and led me back into the ward.

" 'The problem here,' he said, 'is the most complex problem of all. I doubt if we shall really solve it until we are quite certain what the meaning of life is. These patients here—of course, they cannot understand a word we are saying to each other—are, as you noticed, all elderly; some of them are eighty. Further, they are all suffering from—or perhaps I should say, they are all burdened with—tumors. All our diagnostic work has not yet settled that problem: what are these tumors? Are they life or death? Is this a question life is asking of us because it has superior knowledge and wishes us to understand the mystery, the secret of which it knows, or is life itself held up by the problem of general control and asking us to solve for it?'

"As we talked, we strolled from that building to another, some distance away. The one we had left was hushed. The one we approached was a contrast. Before we entered, I realized it wasn't for patients. As we passed through the door the din of healthiness doubled, and we saw that it rose from a bathing pool full of seal creatures and young penguins. They were plunging and diving, rushing around in wonderful underwater, racing, circling and somersaulting until the water seathed and bubbled as though it had been aerated. Every now and then a newcomer rushed out from what I took to be dressing cubicles—though it did seem a little unnecessary for creatures who couldn't be naked and ashamed and for whom the water was as much home as the land—and, just as frequently, someone from the pool slipped from view through one of these small doors.

"We strolled along—the noise was too great for conversation though it was the happiest din I've heard—and, leaving the court, we entered into a second area through a door at the end. This, however, was paved, though the paving was so smooth and polished you might have taken it for a sheet of water. The place was quite as full as the other, but didn't immediately give the same impression of being crowded. That was because everyone was moving with beautiful precision in a single, wonderfully elaborate pattern. The whole company, though it filled the place, was dancing with such ease that the units, flowing in and out of each other, suggested the integration of a great loom in full play.

"When I was in Europe I was once rather keen on the ballet—perhaps you've cared for it? It was a rage once upon a time—well, you should see the kind of choreography that super-seals and penguins can extemporize. The one sort of creature had a sinuousness that, as I've said, I'd never seen before or since in any living body—the other moved with a precision of swing, with a pivotal balance which gave just the right solidity and accent and emphasis to the almost liquid movement of the partners in the pattern. I recovered, however, from my interested surprise and remembered why we were there.

"'A laboratory?' I questioned. 'We were going to see a laboratory, I thought.' He nodded affirmatively and strode on to a third court. Here the population seemed to be older and were not moving about. They were ranged in rows and, here again, the greater part of them were the penguin, or the seal type, though there were occasional examples of other species. But it was the sound, not the sight, that arrested one. They were producing the strangest music I've ever heard. They were—I suppose you'd have to call it—singing. One could pick out a deep whistling, a curious ululation and even odder fluting sounds. The only human music I can at all liken it to is that wonderful thing which Brahms composed toward the end of his life. Do you remember it? It was written, I believe, for the greatest clarinet player of the day.

"Well, when those penguin creatures put up their beaks and let the air flute and bubble from their raised necks, you would hear the strange, desolate, but exultant music which in that clarinet piece always seems to me like the cry, half of triumph half of anguish, that some bird creature, aware of the whole longing of life, might utter. And beside them broke out that baying chorus of the seal creatures. I listened, half-stunned, half-fascinated, till I heard my own tongue quacking in my ear. Yes, this was the laboratory. I looked around, my face expressing what my voice couldn't express in that tide of sound—complete bewilderment. He waved me out, and we went through a door in the farther wall, out to where the quiet countryside waited for us and the sound dwindled.

"As we strolled along he remarked, 'You are surprised at that being a place of research—of course, you only saw half of it.' I thought he was going to say something about my not being a trained observer, but he reassured my vanity by adding, 'I didn't take you into the other side for fear of disturbing the workers themselves.' 'Where were they?' I asked.

" 'In behind those little doors through which you saw the testees passing in and out. You see, first of all, as we know that the organism is a single unit, our work is done not merely on parts of the living creature, but on it as a whole. Furthermore, while we do find out a certain amount when we nurse and heal the old and the injured, naturally, we find out much more if we work on the fit and the young. We study the arch of life from two sides, where it rises and where it declines.'

" 'But,' I asked, 'do you have to keep them so noisily amused while they are waiting for their physical examination?' His third eyelid shot across his eye. 'No,' he answered, and one could almost hear the smile in his voice. 'No, you did really see part of the experiment, not merely the waiting place. We want to study life, he said, not merely when it is up against check, conflict, and defeat. If we are really to know it, we must know it at its highest. So, you see, we have the youngest and freshest in the first two courts and, in the third, those at the peak of their strength.'

" 'But what were they doing, weren't they amusing themselves?' I asked.

" 'Yes, and just as any creature that is really healthy, they were creating, too.'

" 'I don't understand.'

" 'Well, we know that life, even when it is most healthy, is not really at the top of its form unless it is expressing itself, is letting the rhythm in it, the rhythm of which it is made, find utterance in the world round it. Those people you saw were, as it were, tuning themselves up. Then, when each has reached his full tonicity, he runs in. At the other side of those doors are panels, like the one you stood in front of, and there observers are making readings all the time, studying the field of each body, seeing its height of potential. Before starting their exercises they are checked; and against the datum line of their unaroused vitality, the pitch that they can reach when they are in full form is scored. So we get some idea, in terms of a calibration of radiation which I fear I cannot explain in detail to you, of the height of vitality to which we should aspire, of the pitch of consciousness at which we might live. So we hope, in the end, to be able to plot the curve of life and discover the level of intensity of consciousness at which we ought to live if we are to fulfill the life within us during the term in which it manifests itself.'

"I own I was a little puzzled by all this and couldn't quite make out what he was driving at. Was this, I wondered, some queer bid for rejuvenation and perpetual youth? Perhaps he saw there wasn't much use telling me more at that point, for he strolled on in silence for a little while. The path leading toward home, after we had gone a few hundred yards, crossed a level surface covered with small billows of turf.

To break the silence I asked, 'What are those?' thinking they might be some odd, natural formation. 'That—' he remarked over his shoulder, 'that's the cemetery.'

" 'Then you do have death?'

" 'Why not? It isn't death that puzzles us. It is the failure of death to be a natural process. Birth and death balance each other. But as there can be a healthy birth, so there should be a healthy death. And as there can be a very clumsy and dangerous birth, so there can be a clumsy and dangerous death. That is our problem. I think we know the term of life as we know the term of birth. Birds are, perhaps by their nature, more familiar with the mystery of hatching than are mammals. I don't think we should fall easily into the illusion that life, in any one of its forms or its aspects, is complete in that aspect. No, when our people or any of our living wards become old, what we want for them is a clean and healthy delivery into another experience. So, you see, what we are doing in the ward you've just left, the last ward, is not to make these creatures immortal or even to recover but to see how far we can smooth out the knot of life so that they may be easily born and well-born into their next experience.'

"I confess that I never thought about life in quite so comprehensive a manner as that. After a moment's pause I said, 'I thought that you were attempting to make a world here in which everything would be stabilized. I suppose mechanical notions are so firmly fixed in my head that I can't believe you would really trust life as far as death. I thought somehow it would all end happily ever afterward, in a perpetually revolving machine.'

" 'Yes,' he said, and I think he nearly chuckled; I know he put out his hand and touched my shoulder. 'Yes, we don't dictate to life; as its acolytes, we only ask whether we may be permitted to be of assistance. The machine can only repeat, and if we repeated we should be machines and untrue to the stanchless creative mystery of the life within us. All we may hope to do is to bring into consciousness, without thwarting that power, some of its mysterious potentiality.'

" 'Then,' I said tentatively and with a little sense of nervous humor, 'you don't have incubators?'

" 'No,' and now I was sure he chuckled, 'no, we still think that life, when it takes a hand, should be allowed to have its head, and that, if I may go a step further in anatomy, means trusting the heart. You see, we know enough to know how little we know. I can tell you this: there is something superbly mysterious in parenthood. I am not talking from vague speculation. We did experiment, and we found out, as we are always finding out where nature lets us help, and where she has already told us what kind of help she wishes us to give. Something goes on between the parents and the chick even when it is in the egg. Probably it is a radiation which we have not yet "cracked." And like most natural balances it is a real balance. Life, when it is not thwarted, is a very just balancer. What is good for the chick is also good for the parents. They gain something from this fostering period as does their child.'

"This line of thought again gave me almost too much to turn over in my mind. I broke the silence by saying, 'We had a philosopher who started us on our present scientific career, and he said, 'Obey nature in order to rule her.'

"'Yes,' he remarked meditatively. 'Yes, I think that may account for certain things I had gathered about the human race. Certainly our motto would be: "Control nature in order to obey her." Well,' he said after a pause, 'that, you see, is our secret in a nutshell. We have the direct power, as you would say, over life, but, as I would say, to work in with life, to work in the very web of being. Elsewhere intelligent beings can only have an indirect power. And, having this, we don't need anything else. As I have told you, we don't know the end of the story. Perhaps we never shall. But we do know that we are on the way, that we have as much truth as we can grasp, and that it is yielding us the fullness of life.'

"He was silent for a little while, and then he went on in a lighter tone. 'Of course, though our lives look idyllic and simple, you see that, just behind the appearance, is power, the vastest power life has ever known, which till now no form of life has ever been permitted to handle. We expose ourselves to a tornado of pelting force, a force which can take matter to pieces and make flesh rot into a pulp. But, like a carver of hard stone, we may manipulate what we hold in our hands in the cutting stream of this force and, by skilled manipulation make the stream of destruction carve new living forms for us in living tissue, without shedding a drop of blood. We build up what we need or, rather, what we believe life needs from us. We take evolution's slow ideal and, going into the furnace of power, we cast for it what it would have taken millions of years for it to forge on the anvil of events. And when the life process has become thwarted in some blind alley, we draw it back, we remelt it and resupple it and give back the creative power of freedom to those who had all but lost it.'

"He stopped, and, even in his quiet steady quack I thought I caught a slight tremor of emotion, of daring, of sighted triumph. So this was what this odd place was for. This was what these strange creatures, or at least this master creature, lived for. 'One question,' I said, 'How—'

" 'Yes,' he remarked, 'you ought to have that question answered before I put my final one to you. You were going to ask, weren't you, how it is that I know as much as I do?'

" 'Well,' I replied, a little embarrassed, 'of course I am a bit taken aback—'

" 'And of course,' he replied quickly, 'I can't really explain to you how I know, unless you have the kind of mind I have. Mind you,' he went on almost a little hurriedly, 'mind you, I don't want to suggest that your mind has not channels of apprehension far better than mine. But I think it must be clear to you that though we are both warm-blooded animals and so have converged on intelligence, we come to understanding from different sides and so with different insights. I can explain this a little by pointing out that we birds have two gifts that you mammals lack; one is the emotions, and the other is the senses. To be brief, in our development they have chimed. By nature we have a profound sensitiveness, although we ourselves may seem massive and even stolid to you. You must remember that our whole metabolism is faster and our vital heat greater. Our lives are as lengthy as yours, but we live more intensely than you do in the allotted seventy years. Of course, high emotional intuition not governed by intelligence will not lead to understanding, but it is an invaluable spur to the sympathy that is the understanding of the heart. The other thing that adds so greatly to our knowledge is this strange sensory gift. As you know, in all the pigeon family it is present as a sensitiveness to the earth's magnetic field. Their homing instinct is possible by their ability to attend to this frame of reference and so know their bearings. And all the migratory species also carry their own power to apprehend invisible tracks. Now, put those two things together.'

"He turned to me, his head sideways, but I am afraid I looked at him blankly. 'Well,' he said, not wishing to expose my dullness, 'it's quite obvious that if a creature has a profound sensitiveness to emotional states—these, I may tell you, we now know, are a form of radiation—and if he can, through his own nervous system, also pick up the wave lengths of the earth's magnetic field, what would you expect?'

"Again I could only look stupidly expectant.

" 'You are probably aware,' he continued with courteous patience, 'that the homing instinct of birds can be thrown out completely when they fly near a radio station.'

"At last I thought I began to see light. 'Do you mean—?'

" 'That's it exactly,' he said. 'Of course, we can't get words, nor do we need to. But we get the impulses. I have, you see, a very shrewd and, indeed, rather sad view of the progress you, our companions as the advanced scouts of life, have made. And that brings us back to your problem, your place in this.'

"It was a question. It was *the* question. My mind had gone through another of those sudden reversals that, as in the beginning, I had found the most trying element in the strangeness of my adventure. First I had thought them human; then I had thought of them as deadly birds; then I had had to switch back again and realize that they were alternative humans, alternatives to humanity. Now I had gradually, day after day, come to feel that here was an innocent retirement, a real city of refuge, among creatures of a simple virtue and with freedom from all man's problems, childishly ignorant of progress and struggle and adventure and doubt. And now, in a moment, I had to face up to the fact that here were body-minds standing up to risks, under pressures, making experiments, exposed to dangers beside which our old-fashioned revolutions and battlefields were just nursery naughtiness. . . . Again he read my thought, 'I think you're right, and don't feel that I think you're running away. As I have said, I'm not at all sure your physique could stand this mysterious, highly charged climate, and though we, on our part, would be quite ready to let you try, for we should all gain knowledge and we all believe that we—the bird leaders, and you, the mammal leaders, must one day converge and direct the life process in its further advance; yet, it is for you to choose, and your deepest wish may be your soundest guide.'

"As we continued our discussion we had come back to our old places. We were in the administrative building in his inner office. He was pacing up and down with a pendulum's steadiness. I was perched, crouched up in the window niche. We were silent. Then he came over to me and put out his queer massive hand. It was as strong as stone, and one could feel the great vitality in him.

" 'Goodby. I know enough to know that there is no chance or accident. You came here and have learned. And we have learned, too. The process we serve comes from behind all material appearance and thence it returns again. We shall all have learned—all the more if for the moment we don't quite know what to make of this particular piece of knowledge.'

"So I was to go back. I felt, I own, a moment's self-centered relief. It was better to go back to one's own kind than to live with strangers, however kind, however wise. Better to be with one's own than even with the good and the enlightened. But I take a little credit to myself that in the middle of my self-interest there did cross my mind a thought for these extraordinary hosts of mine.

" 'One question,' I said, getting up and feeling a kind of strength come to me just by asking it. But I didn't get far enough to put it into words.

" 'Thank you,' he said, 'I had hoped you would ask that. It is, isn't it? If we let you go out, you will tell the world, and the world will come, and we shall be destroyed.' 'Yes,' I said, 'that's it; that's pretty sure, isn't it?'

" 'I hope we'd let you go,' he said, 'even if the risk were all you think, for why should your side always fail when given knowledge and our side always fail when using trust? But, as it happens, that choice at present is not put before us. No one can enter this place unless we wish it. First of all, no one will ever suspect this place is here.'

" 'But surely they will fly over it?' I asked.

" 'Probably, but if they do, they will look down on such a close cloud pack that they will mistake it for a snowfield.'

" 'But then they'll come across the snow with motor sleds,' I suggested.

" 'No, I repeat. It's impossible for anyone to enter this place unless we wish it. That is one of our simplest initial discoveries, made when we were seeking the balance I told you of, between the radioactivity of parts of the ground here and of the cosmic radiation that pours in on this spot. As you've seen, we use them for our work to balance one against the other. But to prevent intrusion we could use them together. Then no one could enter. The semicircular canals of the ear on which the balance of all mammals depends work through a liquid acting as a spirit level. Tip that to the slightest degree, and it is impossible for the person so touched to stand straight. He has no choice but to lie on the ground in hopeless vertigo. If we direct a band of a particular radiation to the crater rim, no one can cross that frontier, and, if we choose, we have only to alter the wave length a little while he lies there and his whole nervous system will be put out of gear. All memory, all will, and all consciousness, must vanish. But no permanent damage is done. The moment we raise the barrage, the man can recover, though probably he will have a great deal of amnesia and so will not be able to remember why he had come. Of course, if he was too long exposed, his recovery would be dubious.'

" 'You're safe,' I said. 'I think so,' he replied. 'I think life intends us to work on our own a little longer, so that we may have more to give when the time comes for our meeting.'

"And then I saw the third eyelid flutter across that bright, seemingly expressionless eye. 'And of course,' the level quacking went on, 'of course, we have the psychological defense before there will be any need for the defense of advanced physics. You see, if you will run over your story in your mind, you will realize that no one will believe you, anyhow.' "

* * *

"That's the question," said my yarner, suddenly getting up. He put out his hand.

"Well, thank you for letting me tell you my story. No, of course, I don't want anything. I only want you to answer one question; you don't believe a word of it? You're the dozenth person I've told the story to. I tell it once a year, on the anniversary of my ejection from paradise. 'Eden on Ice,' I call my story. You'll own that, beside it, Shangri-La isn't even small beer?"

"Yes," I said anxiously, hurriedly. "Yes, it leaves Tibet and all that cold or tepid or—"

"Yes," he said, "I knew you'd say that; they all do. But the question, you know, isn't that. The question I ask all of them is, just this, DO YOU BELIEVE A WORD OF IT?"

He looked at me with a straining anxiety I found more painful every moment. This man, this harmless nice fellow, desperately wanted me to believe this was a true story. It would mean, literally, an immense amount to him if I could truthfully say I believed it. I tried. The words stuck. It just couldn't be. I didn't have anything to say.

"The bird was a prophet, too," he said. "I didn't know it would mean so much. I think I'd rather have had an albatross around my neck. Good night."

And he was gone. But if he ever had had an albatross around his neck, then I was his wedding guest—certainly after a strange night, in which my dreams were lit by low clouds on which baleful fires flickered and sank.

"A sadder" if not "a wiser man I rose the morrow morn."

"DESPAIR DEFERRED . . . ?"

Miss Potts put down Pollard's summary of Kretschmer's *Psychophysical Types.* For the fifth time she had read the passage beginning, "The Picnic type invariably associates a full and rounded physique with a cheerful, resilient disposition." But, as her eye scanned the line, her ear listened to something quite different. It continued to echo with something she had been discussing half an hour ago when she had left the common room.

Miss Potts was not "Picnic." She was hawklike. Her body was not upholstered so as to be resilient. Her forte was not bounce, but grip. Indeed, her mind, like a bird's claws, once it had taken hold, found it very hard to let go. She was tall, distinguished, her friends said, and she sometimes said it to herself when trying to arrange herself in front of the mirror. She whispered it only to stop the other whisper which she knew her not-friends sometimes exchanged: that she was gaunt; "awfully nice, of course, but really rather overtense, don't you think?" After all, it's no use simply waiting to bounce back if you are not pneumatic. You've just got to hang on and see that you are not pelted off your perch. But then you must fix your mind and not let it slip. She must concentrate her attention on this science of personality. That would give her detachment. Perhaps she'd do better with the passage about the type nearest her own. She turned to the description of the Asthenic type. It was—in its successful examples—very retentive. It didn't just bob up and come back. This type stuck it out. But then, of course, it could concentrate its attention. And that, it was quite clear, Miss Potts couldn't do.

This time she didn't even put the book down. She simply let it sag on her lap. Her eyes went out of focus; her ear, like a badly adjusted phonograph, slipped back into the old groove of the record and ground out the same passage with exasperating repetition. "Well" (what a queer word with which to start things, last fossil of an extinct optimism), "well, it's really all up. We've got to face facts. There's nothing more we can do." She had come away from the common room when for the third time the discussion, so affable and so futile, so reasonable and frank on the surface, so just-under-the-surface panicky, had come around to that helpful conclusion.

The common room at Batscombe School was, Miss Potts was used to thinking, perhaps the best clearinghouse for intelligent views in the whole country. When she had joined the school staff she had felt that, in a way, she had reached, if not the top of the tree, at least quite a remarkable elevation. Where else would you meet birds of so many feathers, of such wide ranges of flight, and so voluble? Everything was discussed: nothing was taboo. Here was the peak of progressive education.

Miss Potts came from St. Margaret's, Oxford. She was the elder daughter of a widowed lawyer, who had been proud of his angular child. "Bits of her mind," he used to say to himself, "are almost a man's." So, when she wanted to take up education seriously, off she went to Oxford. Yet Oxford didn't quite do. The air, ten years ago, had been full of rumors that the older universities were really out of date. Miss Potts threw in her lot with the Progressives. Oxford even scorned psychology. So, once the break was made, Miss Potts went all out for Freud and Freedom. But though bits of her mind may have been masculine, nearly all her body was feminine. However progressive, the mixture is very seldom conducive to peace of mind. Miss Potts wanted to be free, but free for what? Free to be alone? Hardly; indeed, to be frank, not at all. Free, of course, to find linking easy. And that was far more easily said than done. Even when she had settled in Batscombe—with the highest if most discreetly screened hopes—she found, at least for herself, at least for distinguished women with largely masculine minds, that there was a great deal more talking than doing. Again and again, as she brightly, candidly, openly discussed the psycho-physical problem with some very intelligent young male master—for Batscombe was, of course, rigidly coeducational—she saw what a gap yawned between words and acts. Indeed, as she pressed on (for wasn't she a psychologist, trained to observe?), she could not doubt that she saw in young Harold's face that slight rigidity of the cheek muscles which unmistakably indicate the stifled but all-the-more exhausting yawn and, even worse, that slight swivel of the eye as that young, none-too-well-educated Miss Brown ran in laughing loudly.

After three years Miss Potts had discussed the whole of life with everyone. And, as far as it meant living, as far as it meant having any more actual experience than at an Anglican girls' school, it was just as though she had never been a Progressive, had never read a line of Freud, had never discussed anything but topics proper to a maiden aunt. This, at Batscombe, was serious. That is not to say it was not a laughing matter. That was precisely why it was so serious. For, if you did not have an affair at Batscombe, it was almost as bad as though, at a good old-fashioned "finishing school," your French accent was too English. Those whose accent and idiom were perfect made amusing little *mots* about you behind your back. Yet Batscombe was in the first flight of progress and Miss Potts had gone on drawing an astringent comfort from that. Granted, she might not have made the grade among the residents themselves, yet there she was. The intellectual, scholastic world, if unwillingly, looked up to Batscombe, she was sure, and anyone on its staff was a distinct figure, above the crowd. And even if you could not cash in on all the liberties you preached, well, after all, wasn't there something finer in that anyhow? Though you might not get any of the beer, you could play skittles with other pompous people's convictions and scornfully tell them what you thought of their "opium."

Indeed, once or twice, when she had been asked during vacations to address small groups of inquirers at Hampstead, she had tried (and brought off, she believed), as a sort of peroration for Progressives, those long passages from Shaw and Russell. One was G.B.S.'s aphorism: He who seeks for new liberties for others will not, before they are openly granted for all, prejudice his case with the public by prematurely availing himself of a special license. She culminated with "Bertie's" grand slam: "Only on the Foundation of an unyielding Despair can the Soul's habitation be built."

The fact remained, however, that progressive educators and B.R., Freud, and Kretschmer, and Batscombe to a man, and woman didn't really believe in a soul at all. They believed in mind-bodies; and frankness and truth, their twin god, compelled one to add that the accent was wholly on the body. A soul was the state of mind of a rationally satisfied body. And Miss Potts, in that searching sense, had been far from satisfied. Indeed, things had come to such a pass that, after an effort at psychoanalysis and another at endocrine dosage and a third at orthostasis, Miss Potts very quietly, but all the more broodingly, began to think of opium. Not of the druggist's variety, of course. Her digestion had never been her strong point; she hated sticking needles into herself and her hangover of Oxford good taste still made her feel a reactionary disgust when younger members of the faculty became tipsy. The opium, she, daughter of "dreaming spires," began to hanker for was religion.

So it was that she faced the middle years. It was not a cheerful outlook. Often she felt acutely miserable. Sometimes she thought in a sort of adolescent, melodramatic way of suicide, that sort of suicide in which you are not the "demmed damp body" but an onlooker at the sympathetic and shocked onlookers, hearing all their remorse-stricken eulogies and following a handsome funeral to a charmingly situated grave.

And then came the war. That certainly raised the pressure from the personal front. It also brought relief for all the Progressives. They had been against war. It was part of the new creed that war was simply due to sex-repression. Sex, being unrepressed by Progressives, they naturally maintained that they had debunked war and they dismissed it with a laugh. But this war was different. It was present, pressing. The enemy was obviously suffering frightfully from sex-repression. The free, unrepressed peoples must unite now to oppose and end this sex-repression. So the Progressives found themselves freed from their awkward loyalty to peace, which, anyhow, was only a by-product of being unrepressed. After all, if little Alec is permitted to hit Susie on the head for fear he'd grow up repressed if he didn't, surely if I have been repressed during childhood—not allowed to kick and bite father and mother—I had better get it out of my system now, especially when the enemy is so reactionary and would never permit children their charter right to kick their elders.

And it worked. During those first months of the "waiting war" there had been a new friendship between the school and the town and country, which at first had been very cold to this new intrusion. Now all was warm and friendly. There was also, not less warming, a new friendship in the school itself. Those common room meetings, from which Miss Potts had for some time come away feeling out of the fun and the frank talk, now held her; she was wanted and she wanted to stay on. The young ones wanted to hear about the last war. She and her contemporaries compared experiences, were listened to as they showed how the present war was different from the last one; how right all of them were then to protest, how right now, to co-operate. And, best of all, there was a new truce in Miss Potts herself. A full sex life or religion ceased to be the only choice, the horned dilemma. A third way opened: the life of devoted action—clear, progressive thought, framing a really lasting peace. Everyone of intelligence was wanted now, and there could be complete accord and understanding with the dear old Church, which, after all, was doing its bit, and far from a little bit, by keeping up morale and keeping war aims high.

But that was only during the "waiting war," while one sighed vicariously for poor Poland, read all about concentration camps—as a duty to keep the edge of one's resolution whetted—and, when one went to town, carried, with a sense of humorous seriousness, one's little neatly satcheled gas-mask. Month by month one became acclimatized to the war. It was clear this war was going to be a repetition of the last. The poor Poles were obviously unready. The West would, however, be rigid. Jokes about the blitz that failed to burst were clichés.

Then came May. For weeks you simply couldn't get your bearings. Everything seemed to be going from under you. After all, war is war, and you had accepted it, surely. But if you did make that sacrifice, then war should keep the rules the experts had said were followed. The soldiers had said it was grim but, in its way, law-abiding. But this thing was nothing you could call by any name you knew. It was not a battle or a siege. It was an obliterating deluge, a human typhoon. You saw it, hour after hour, sweeping away everything: impregnable defenses, inviolable countries, unbreakable alliances—everything went down into the maelstrom. You still ate food, but it tasted like damp paper. If you slept, your dreams seemed worse than being awake—until you awoke. The sun shone—"June's blue weather"! Why couldn't it rain! "A night in June"! Oh, for a blizzard!

And now, today, Miss Potts had left the common room as early as she used to leave it before the war. Then, on those days, she'd often felt she couldn't be more unhappy, more unhappy, with less to live for: leaving all those silly, gay, date-making young people—yes, and some of them, her age, still doing it successfully; she, who had never even started. . . . And now, though they had all been friendly, yes, pathetically friendly; though they had all been tied together as never before—one of the young ones, handsome as those T.B. cases often are, had actually said, "I envy you your age; you've lived and had the good years"—still, she had to get away. For everyone now agreed that it was all up. It was really no more than a matter of days. The new mechanized military machine would just continue to sweep over everything. The very latest of fortifications had not stood against it; why should our dear old-fashioned fleet? All defenses would be air-bombed out of existence.

And then? She had looked forward so dolefully to the prospect of long, unchanging, empty years ahead of her. How utterly stupid that kind of expectation seemed now! How ridiculous those "better dead" wishes appeared. Indeed, what wouldn't she now give just to feel again that basic security in which one could believe that one's own love-life mattered. She had thought herself desperately ill-used because, lying awake in her warmed room on her spring mattress, she was, as Sappho had cried, "alone." Now, how long could she hope to have any privacy left her? She remembered every detail of what she had read about the concentration camps, had read, she now realized, not to get ready for one herself, but to steel herself to tell the boys she had taught that now they must man the planes that must beat the enemy peoples till they compelled their tyrant leaders to make peace. Today all that dreadful reading had quite another meaning.

As she looked down into the little valley at the bottom of which she could see the sea shining in the sunlight, there flashed into her mind the picture of a horrid woodcut in an old *History of England* which she had read as a child. It showed the nuns of Whitby Abbey in Yorkshire gathered together by their Abbess. There was a basin on the table around which they stood. The caption was: "At the approach of the Danes, the nuns, to save themselves from a worse fate, instructed by their abbess, took each in turn a razor and cut off their noses and their lips." As a child, she had laughingly shuddered at such a conventual defense. But now? Would not death be better than capture, insult, confinement, torture?

For years she had played with suicide possibilities. If one had an incurable disease? If one was in a bad accident? If one was caught in a burning house? Taking out of her pocket the key that she always carried, she went to her locked drawer. Yes, there was the small bottle.

She remembered one day some summers ago. She had been in the biological laboratory; one of the butterfly-killing bottles had been dropped by its owner, a boy of fourteen. Being a good Progressive, he had called out, "Oh, I say, Potty, I've broken that bloody killing-bottle. Do be a peach and help me clear it up." She then set him to picking up the scattered pieces of glass. The cake of cyanide itself had split.

One half lay out on the floor. The other had rolled under the laboratory bench. She stooped down to where she thought it must be, then reeled, and found herself sitting with her back against the wall.

The reek of almonds, the migraine split in the brain—she knew enough chemistry to know what had happened. A glance showed that she had had only a whiff. A crumb of the cake had fallen into a few drops of water under the bench. Hence the sudden mouthful of gas that had knocked her out. The boy had gone, leaving her to clear up.

"That's just like all these Progressives," she remembered thinking, "an old maid, old Potty can finish up the mess they make, and be finished off for all they care."

A sudden hatred of life had swept her and with it an instant sense of how easy it was to end it all. "So every bondsman in his own hand bears the power to cancel his captivity." She got up carefully, carefully collected the cyanide in one of the wide-mouthed, glass-stoppered bottles.

It was this bottle that she now drew out. She knew what to do: take the soap dish, put enough water in it just to cover the bottom of it, crumble the cyanide. Then empty the paper into the water, as she sat on the floor with her face over it, like the Delphic Sibyl snuffing up the laurel fume. It would all be over in less than five seconds. She wouldn't know anything after the first couple. She went through the steps in her mind. It was all so simple, practical, fool-and-knave-proof. Here was ultimate armor, a fortified line which was impregnable. She realized, with a distinct relief, that just by thinking this out and making up her mind about what to do, she had gained a sort of reprieve.

She felt a wave of dignity and detachment swell in her. It rose, she told herself, from winning back the initiative against life. She was no longer a whimpering rabbit running hopelessly from the pursuing weasel. She was at bay, and being at bay meant that you turned; and, once you had turned, you could judge the precise distance between yourself and your pursuer.

She remembered someone saying that it was hope that hurt; full despair was an anesthetic. Certainly, now with the poison bottle out in her hand and the method thought out, she felt quite secure, actually, at her ease.

She had time. They were still on the other side of the Channel. Of course, they would be on this side sometime during the month. There must be no nonsense of hope revived. That would be like letting circulation come back into an anesthetized limb. But, before they came, there was pretty certainly a fortnight ahead, perhaps more than that.

So the next thing she must do was fix a dead line. She went over to the window. When those troops appeared down in the village—when it was quite clear—then she'd reconnoiter like this from the window, she'd turn back to the room, and go through her rite with the soap dish. She had time till the enemy captured Batscombe. That, she reflected again, was certainly a fortnight off. Quite time enough, if you didn't eat, to become so weak that by then you'd hardly care who came.

So, since all arrangements were made and there was really nothing more to do, one had better have lunch. Still, you never knew what surprise might be sprung—a raider squadron from the sky, for instance. Pop a piece of cyanide in your mouth, and that would serve quite as well as the planned inhaling. Though, if there was time enough, she was set on having her ritual, still, just against "eventualities," she took her bottle with her.

Every noon, though, she would come back to her room. The news remained frightful. True, the central blow was rearing over their heads; but meanwhile right and left any possible side supports were dashed away. Therefore, after the daily meeting at the common room, Miss Potts retired to her own room. She would first take out the bottle; then she would look down through the glass stopper into its little shaft. She called it her evacuation route. It contained a magic mushroom like the one Alice in Wonderland had to eat to get through the tiny door into that other world. She would then take the soap dish, solemnly place it on the floor, fetch the water bottle, kneel down, carefully pour in the specified amount until the bottom of the dish was covered, and then, placing the poison bottle just the other side of the dish, she would turn and loosen the glass stopper. Yes, it moved easily enough. She could see the yellow-white paste inside. Indeed, as she bent over, she could smell the almond flavor distinctly.

Since the news refused to get better, and yet the climax, the actual invasion, refused to emerge, the drill had to be continued. Miss Potts had begun it just to be sure that she would know all the moves without slip or fail when, in a fortnight or three weeks hence, she would actually carry it out. The three weeks became three months, and still the blow was just as imminent. The ax was upraised over the victim's neck, so it was silly to take one's head off the block. Yet Time itself, Miss Potts began to discover, is something, even when the events which should keep time won't turn up according to schedule. She went through the daily rite and it still fortified her. There was just as much reason for going on with it as when it was begun, just as much reason for being ready for "a fate worse than death." More countries were going under the machine and more populations were engulfed. Their cries rose out of the daily paper megaphoned by propaganda. She was never permitted to forget. But something else was creeping into her drill. It was becoming something of an end in itself—more ritual than drill. As, day by day and week by week, she withdrew to what she was now calling her boat drill, as torpedoed ships and fear of starvation by blockade began again to figure more in the press and in talk than the invasion itself, she found dread beginning to fade, to modulate—she could hardly believe it—almost into disappointment.

The first time she recognized it was when, as the first step in her ritual, after she had locked her door, she went to the window to make her official inspection of the village street a mile away and to draw down the sash. Her rule ran: When, on looking down to the main street, it is seen to be empty of all save those deadly gray or black uniforms, then the rite is to be completed and the "mystery celebrated." But, as she looked down at the village, she realized she could scarcely see it, so misty was it; and the near-by trees at which she glanced were almost leafless. A whole season was gone. The dreadful, incongruous beauty of summer had vanished. The protective fog and cloud were here.

Still, the news *was* desperate. She could not stop her practice. In the common room several people had remarked that she really seemed quite serene. She knew on what her serenity was founded; she put her hand on the little bottle concealed in her dress. Gradually, though, even the common room's tone began to change. In June, Stetson, the mathematics master, had said, "Well, I'm having my bottle of '92 port tonight—not going to let those brutes spill that, too." But now he had just told them what care he was taking of a small cabinet in which he protected his last dozen cigars from damp. "Never get any more of those till hell knows when."

Of course, though, it was only a reprieve, and the reprieve was really a ruse. She wasn't going to be caught. There was not the slightest ground for hope, and, if she admitted hope again, she would have to go through its deadly sickness and death again. No, once bitten, twice shy. She would keep up her ritual. She would not let the local anesthetic fail; she would not let feeling come back again.

So she fought the insidious invader threatening to sap her defenses and lure her from her impregnable lines. For a long time, therefore, nothing disturbed her life. She refused to look at the calendar. There was only one event which could again start time for her. She didn't read the papers, but she knew that nothing had changed—the situation was still so desperate that it was only to be confronted by the attitude she had taken up. At the back of her mind, though, the faintest questioning went on like those telephone conversations sometimes heard on long-distance, so faint that a word can be heard only here and there. She had rewon the initiative, the initiative to turn around and face life. What then? Wasn't life itself going on? Was that enough? Did it give you enough initiative, just to turn around and face a pursuer who wouldn't come up?

Of course, she did her wartime duties as well as her school

work. But the former was no more defense against inner defeat than the latter. No, the only defense was to know, to demonstrate daily—ritually, as she did, alone by herself—that hope was dead, that there was nothing to fear, because hope, fear's accomplice, was being duly and daily certified as dead and buried.

She was meditating over this on her knees one day, with the soap dish with its water in it, the bottle with its stopper "officially" loosened till you could just smell almonds, when she noticed that her tongue, running idly around the inside of her mouth, had found a cavity in the back of one of the lower bicuspids. She hadn't been to the dentist for months—she was due for a routine inspection just at the time that time stopped. But, of course, she couldn't go now; that wouldn't do. Utterly inconsistent. Why keep up roof repairs in a house you have mined and mean to blow up the moment a long-expected event materializes? Through that small repaired cavity hope and the reacceptance of life would steal in on its own terms and not on one's own rational conditions. Even if the tooth ached, it would be a constant reminder to her not to forget, not to settle down again. Even if it was septic—well, death by premature aging was perhaps kinder and better for everyone than the cyanide way—if there was time. One thing was clear: just the wish to avoid natural death should not lure her back to going on with life-at-any-cost.

Then, there was Simpkins at the farm. She remembered vividly how he had said to her, that day she'd given up hope and resolved to die, "I'm fifty, Miss, but good for another twenty years, and to think I'd have to live out my life under *them!* I've got to stick to the farm. It's my skilled way of keeping them out. But, by George, if I see them in these fields with their dirty boots on my land, I'll pitchfork the first couple like stooks, right over the hedge. I'm as strong as any lad of twenty-five." And he was. Yet she had suddenly been called into the farmyard as she was going along the lane that led from the school buildings to her rooms.

There he lay. He had been pitching straw; the pitchfork was still stuck in a truss. He was down in the straw, his strong, worn left hand clawed against his chest. "Lord," he panted, "Lord." She saw at once that he mightn't last till the Doctor came, and, naturally, she had no injections with her—only her precious bottle. It wasn't much help. She knelt beside him.

"You've done your bit grandly," she said. It was all she could think of.

His eyes rolled around to hers. "What," he whispered.

"You've helped, as much as anyone, all of us, to resist."

Then she thought she had better add something stronger to help him in his deafening pain.

"You've helped us to win." He'd never be there to see, one way or the other.

"To win?" he whispered; puzzled, querulous. "God, is Doctor coming?"

"Yes," she said, "yes, he's just here."

Suddenly the clawed hand opened. Simpkins spoke very faintly but without strain. "Whew, that was hell," he said. "Lord, I'm comfortable . . . but weak, awfully weak."

Then, with surprise all the more intense because it seemed to be conveyed from such an immense distance, as he spoke in the thinnest whisper, "What's this? *What's* this?" His mouth fell open with what seemed ultimate amazement. He was dead.

And he was her age, much stronger, of course, too. Last June, if anyone had said, "Which of those two would go first?" she surely would have been the choice. So time did go on. Men wore out and died, just as they did when there was no war. She found that she had come to think that you simply couldn't die unless you were killed or you killed yourself. And here, right at her feet, was death at his work, taking his average yield. And his partner, pain, worked beside him just as efficiently without bayonet or bastinado, and just as though gas and bombs weren't needed to make life intense and to make time count.

That noon, as she knelt before her bowl of "happy dispatch," her mind wandered beyond her bicuspid cavity. These two things, her fate and the country's defeat—the one entailing death for the other—no longer seemed to embrace everything between them. They really didn't go down—as she had assumed—to the foundations of everything. Something else went on underneath, like an immense ocean current on which all the sea wrack, foam, and waves, churned and floated.

Still, for the time being, the war and its overarching breaker must be all, for all of them under its shadow. She must be ready to plunge at a moment's notice. She could not and she would not withdraw her ultimatum. She could and would accept life only on her own terms: victory or death. Surely there could no longer be any doubt about that. That was the only possible Realism. Yes, in Simpkins' death one saw that life was going on its own way and, of course, victory would and could mean only death deferred. "We all live under an indefinite reprieve." Who had said that? Wasn't it one of those comfortable Victorians whose security and firm expectation of living seemed almost fabulous now? Yet the daily news always reconfirmed her grim faith. She would quote Chesterton. "I bring you nought for your comfort: Yea, nought for your desire: Save that the sky grows darker yet: And the sea rises higher." The storm must, it simply must, sooner or later blot out everything. About that there could be no doubt. And that was the issue, the only issue for practically everyone. Of course, some hundreds, thousands—if the suspense could really be sustained—might go as Simpkins had gone; slipping out in the pause before the blow. They must go by the law of averages, but they would only be those exceptions which prove nothing.

She thought rapidly of the national statistics she had read: some five hundred thousand people died "from natural causes" every year. That number would represent a big battle, even today. But, of course, they were nearly all old or very young. And what were the latest figures about fewer people in the island dying by accident because, in spite of the great number butchered by bombs, the check on the motor traffic had greatly reduced the road casualties? Somehow one had never thought of the civilian's motor car as a monster destroying life. Yet there it had been, a worse Juggernaut than many a tank.

Simpkins' last moment kept on coming back to her. She could hear his voice, passionate and strong last June, utterly involved in the one issue, victory or death; and then across that resolute tone she heard the thin whisper cutting through all that assurance. When he was actually dying, all he had said, about dying with brave good faith, meant just nothing. It all melted away in something far bigger that underflowed it.

Yet she wasn't dead; wasn't likely to be, soon. The one likelihood, the one pretty certainty (how odd to call such a degree of high risk by that vapid little word "pretty"), the one thing they must all still count on, was the invasion, and then, when it came off, then she must do her bit and call in death.

So the ritual was continued right into the spring, and outwardly it continued to be fully sanctioned. People came down regularly from Town, half stunned. The preliminary barrage for the invasion, one could see, was being kept on at full blast. Life surely was hell; and though one might "stick it out," one could never think of lessening, even by a jot, one's minimum terms. There they stood, starkly rational: victory, or defeat and death. If it was victory, then one would reconsider the terms on which one might take back the deceiver. But to think of victory was to let hope get its nose out of the bag and begin to breathe again.

The facts, the bare facts without a shred of wishful thinking, came just to this: Though a few irrelevant deaths—a sort of seepage—might go on, for practically everyone everything else had stopped or had ceased to matter. Time had stopped, for all private life had stopped, arrested until the Great Event on which it would be decided whether life again would ever be livable. Of course, some private affairs did go on. Now and then, people were married—just as now and then, the older ones died. But in its way marriage was simply—like any other rations—an aid to one's war work. Relaxation, concerts, movies, dances, these were all part of mental and physical hygiene, and so was marriage. Of course, no one could. . . .

And then Adelaide, her only first cousin, whom she had treated as a younger sister, called suddenly, without notice. Adelaide, she remembered, as though in another life, had married during the "gray war," the war of waiting. They hadn't seen each other or heard of each other during this next life, the life of accepted death, death as an everyday possibility. Now, the moment Adelaide stepped into the room, Miss Potts knew that she had no need to be told. She made the easy calculation instantly.

"But," she stammered, and couldn't help herself, "but you must have done it that very month! How could you!"

Adelaide burst into tears and was actually out of the room before Miss Potts realized that, as "elder sister," she had failed in an immemorial "actor-proof" part. She ran out and dragged the girl back.

"I'm so glad," she managed to say.

She noticed her own flat tone and noticed, as clearly, that it had failed to register on the pregnant mother. Her cousin turned with a kind of animal satisfaction, brute, insensitive to all but its own race-enforced impression of life.

"I knew you'd be delighted. Jim and I are so pleased. We're sure it'll be a boy. We've made all the arrangements. The doctor says it's as easy as appendicitis now. Anyhow, just think, when he's born. . . . Oh, I'm so happy!"

Yes, Miss Potts remembered having read all about the endocrine glands and what they do during pregnancy. But now, at this crisis, at this culmination of crises, to bring into this world, into this beleaguered, bombed, invasion-threatened, crowded island, to bring another life, another mouth, to fill another hospital bed . . . !

And Adelaide had been so keen-minded, yes, even to being hard-boiled. She'd been the first to mock propaganda and blah. She was for the war, of course, but only because, as she used to say, if there was a fight, she liked the gloves off. "Call butchery butchery" she used to say coldly. "We've got to clean up the bloody mess. If we fail, we'll be done, and we'll deserve it. If we succeed, well, then we'll get out the old virtues again and see if we can make something efficient out of them this time." Yes, here was the body which a few months ago had uttered all that and much more good, telling, Progressive pitchforking. And now here she was, a cow, big, swollen, diffuse, drugged.

It was later than she thought. Adelaide stayed to tea. Jim, she said, had to be in the district and had left it to her to tell her "sister" the good news. He'd call back. Exercise was all the thing nowadays in pregnancy, right up to the date. And it was, literally, up to the date. Tea was hardly begun—they had hardly taken their first sip of that hay-and-hot-water that now passed for tea—when Adelaide said she felt a little queer.

Miss Potts' anxiety was a good diagnostician. She ran to the telephone. Fortunately, Dr. Charles was at home. He did not come, however, until she had had her second treatment in detachment from the horned dilemma, Victory or Death. She saw Adelaide before her eyes, as she had seen Simpkins; torn out of the present setting, the crisis, rushed, in a moment, out of what had seemed to them all the world of basic realism and plunged into something vaster and deeper. But whereas Simpkins had been snatched by Death, had gone off into some vast unknown, Adelaide, infinitely more puzzling, was being snatched by Life, for something more instant and actual than any simply man-made activity like war.

Here at her knees, instead of her hard-boiled adequate, war-minded cousin, was simply an animal that writhed and bellowed in contest, not with a mortal enemy but with the remorseless drive of Life itself; Life that was so much more agonizing than Death and yet was what people always chose rather than Death: Life that rent and tore, mired and bestialized until, beside this exhibition of birth, a concentration camp seemed an austere, cleanly, monastic order. Even Adelaide's face seemed to be smudged out, all personal expression and character gone, while her body seemed a shapeless bag within which some violent animal was kicking and pounding to break its way out.

And when Dr. Charles took over, the second act was not less surprising, not less incongruous with that attitude which she had built up and taken as Basic Realism. The child emerged, as all children have always emerged, with more outrageous assault on the decencies of every one of the five senses than a massacre could make. But that was not the final shock. That was psychological, not physical. That was Adelaide's reaction. She lay gasping, sweating, swabbed. The billowing smell of chloroform gave a final wash of nausea to the rank farm odors that lay heavily about the room. And, sunken in all this, Adelaide, the neat, the repressed, lay sprawled. Her body might well be out of kilter after such an extraction. It was not the physical sprawl that hit Miss

Potts. It was the idiotic, loose amiability on Adelaide's face; it had become all unstitched, unupholstered.

Dr. Charles was tidying up. After sending Miss Potts to call for a nurse and hearing that none could be along for an hour or more, he said ritually, turning to the patient, "The little chap is doing fine and you're all right, my girl."

Adelaide, who had never seen the doctor before, nodded, smiled sheepishly, and goggled.

"Miss Potts," he said, "give her the boy."

She picked up the object wrapped in a piece of wool, looking, she thought, rather like a large bandaged thumb, and which, a few moments before, she had been ridding of the really quite terrible, natural traveling wrap in which it had arrived. The bath had uncovered an unutterably ancient and wrinkled little fellow: not young, but also not weak. He looked as tough as well-cured rubber and, heavens, he needed to be, considering what she had just seen him go through. He was cross, of course, cross as hell, but he gave a curious sense of vitality and of a settled determination to endure this outrageous experience.

She carried him over to his mother. Adelaide's sagged and damp face—like an energetic washerwoman's held too long over scalding suds—broke into subrational delight. She folded the stirring lump of terra-cotta flesh into her neck. In Miss Potts, only two emotions remained. One expressed itself in the words she whispered to herself, "So this is life, real life—it just doesn't care a damn for meaning—it cares so much that it knows meaning doesn't matter." The other was too strong, too outrageous for words. She felt herself bent over the two creatures who at teatime had still been one; and now one of them would go on into a world she would never know, in which she'd be only the faintest of fading memories at best.

"Goo, goo," she said, "goo, goo."

It was several days before Miss Potts had the use of her sitting room, since Adelaide couldn't be moved to the hospital earlier. Now, "mother and child were doing finely," and, with that bulletin fixed, life and the crisis and the ritual reply-to-the-crisis must be resumed.

Sure enough, the crisis was still there. News continued to be bad; just steadily getting graver; another country had gone under. But, still, the denouement was postponed. It's just like the Arabian Nights, thought Miss Potts. She stood by the window. She ought to be making a survey of the village street (part of the ritual). You could see it beautifully today. She noticed that the trees were in leaf again, as full as when "time officially stopped" last year.

A whole year . . . "a Thousand-and-One-Nights," the famous title came into her mind. So Scheherazade had gained a thousand-and-one reprieves. Three years, she thought. And that started another old, mental echo: "Three years, or the duration of the war." That was the old enlistment term of the last war. That had seemed to last forever, and no one seemed likely to survive it or, if they did, to find any life worth living at the end of it. But now all that was getting on for a quarter of a century ago. People thought about it mainly now, as her parents did about the Crimean war. . . . And in the end Scheherazade was reprieved "for good," indefinitely, and married the monster and gave him a son. . . .

Her mind hopped over to Adelaide. The boy had a name now, Franklin . . . the scientist . . . the explorer . . . the president. He was a registered person. He was growing, too, every day. It was absurd but undeniable; and absurd and undeniable, it was far more interesting than the war news.

She had moved to her washstand and, by routine, had taken the soap dish, removed the soap from its strainer, put the dish on the floor, knelt, poured the water, and then felt in her pocket for the bottle. Of course, she remembered, while Dr. Charles was about, she had locked it up. She did not want his keen nose smelling out that telltale almond scent. She found the key and went to the drawer in her desk. Then she paused.

How long would she go on with this if nothing happened; or, rather, if the zero hour refused to strike though everything else struck and crashed? How long would she wait about, arrested, while Life and Death inexhaustibly dealt out fresh cards in their endless game? Her tongue went to that small bicuspid cavity. Yes, it was twice the size, and the tip of her tongue, like a finger on an electric bell, could start a trill of pain when she pressed in. Was she going to loose that tooth? Here was a small sharp question. She could decide that; she must; she alone would pay if she didn't. After all, death by dental neglect would hardly be realism, and it would be very uncomfortable and slow.

Philosophers had endured prison, but Shakespeare said even they bowed to toothache. If only things would run on schedule. If only the invasion had been tried and failed—or had come off. But just as it was—with some people dying and others being born just as though the war was not the final thing, and the war always failing to go according to timetable. . . .

Could it be true that just facing things wasn't enough? Might true wisdom be, even, to refuse to face things, to refuse all plans, all large provisions? How could you plan if you couldn't really foresee?

She had thought the actual Gospels pretty soft stuff. They kept her from joining the Church, even when she saw that Christianity in its time, had picked up a lot of psychological knowledge useful enough to stranded individuals. But the Sermon on the Mount; all that sentiment about easygoing lilies and careless little birds. . . ! What was the actual phrase in which all that poetry ended?

As a matter of fact, she remarked to herself as she recalled the passage, it doesn't conclude that everything is sweet fun. The deduced proposition is "Sufficient unto the day is the *evil* thereof." That would mean that one is meant to take life in the actual, swallowable, daily doses as they come.

What had all of them been going through? They had been trying to stop the present and to live in what they had concluded was a certain future. They had been "doing time," as convicts say. But what time? "The indeterminate sentence." She smiled wryly as that phrase, beloved of progressive penologists, came to her lips. But the meaning of the indeterminate sentence was to give back the initiative to the convict. He could rewin his liberty by doing something, even while doing time. Time, even in prison, waited on you, on your good conduct. No, they had not been going through a progressive, indeterminate sentence—quite the reverse. Something quite different from you and your terms, ultimata, and demands, "controlled the stretch," played the music slow or fast.

Something she'd read in her old college days, when she'd met a Theosophist, floated into her mind. "Time is all," it ran, "Pain and Pleasure, Sorrow and Happiness, Disaster and Prosperity: they are the same thing felt at a different Tempo." Well, she'd heard the psychophysiologists say something of that sort about pain. Her tongue gingerly felt around the back of the bicuspid. You could make the pain go from half-pleasure to quite-pain.

The highbrow hymn went on: "The sum of pain is ever the same. Man calls it happiness when the vast Wheel moves too slowly for him to perceive it. Brahman accelerates the beat and man cries out 'Disaster.' But it is only and always the Wheel." That was probably true, too. Hadn't she often read in animal psychology that most creatures can't notice movement if it is below a certain pace. The Wheel—a pleasant stretch at the pace we are accustomed to but breaking us if it goes any faster. Wasn't that as near the actual truth, "real realism," as one could get, and weren't Christ's practical epigrams the deduced behavior based on such an insight?

After all, everyone does die, whatever you may do; and if life had no sense in itself, it didn't have any more at eighty than at eighteen. Just managing to live long doesn't prove anything. To die an imbecile at eighty or of cancer at seventy, though one might do it in a fine white ward all by oneself—was that a better demonstration of worth-whileness than dying all together, all under forty, in a blind hot belief that Right, our Right, was winning? But we just don't notice the one-by-one erosion. It's the sudden slump of a mass that startles us. We don't notice anything that steals on us.

She had moved back to the window. So out of time had she become that she'd neglected the second part of her ritual; after looking down to the village she should have closed the window. As she raised her free hand to the sash, her eye was caught by something moving very slowly in the undergrowth of the coppice which here came right up to the house.

Yes, it was a cat moving like a shadow. It was stalking, stalking that bird which was picking up worms under the cake of old leaves. The beast stole out of cover, but so steadily that, though the bird between pecks gave its involuntary look around, its eye passed over this quietly changing blur.

She was watching the cat. Now it had ceased to move at all. She could see its shoulder muscles gently folding and mounting under its black fur. The cat was ready to spring. Miss Potts involuntarily flung at it the object in her hand. The cat leaped wildly. The bird squawked away into safety. The bottle had disappeared, but Miss Potts could see the glass stopper gleaming among some leaves.

The damp woodland, she thought, will suck up that bit of poison paste. Perhaps a few grubs will die, and, in consequence, a few saplings will grow better.

She left the window open, picked up the soap dish as she passed it, and replaced it. There were still five minutes before her next class. She'd have time to ring up the dentist and make an appointment.

THE SWAP

"Let's try!"

"What nonsense!"

"Well, if it's nonsense, no harm's done by trying. Besides, it takes only a few minutes anyhow."

"It's too silly—all this Indian pretense."

"But it *isn't* Yoga; it's Sufi. And it's quite plain and experimental. If it doesn't work, we'll know it in five or ten minutes; that isn't much time to lose."

"And if it does?"

"Oh, you own it might!"

"I don't own anything—I mean, I don't allow anything. It's you who want to make this absurd experiment. All I ask is: If such a grotesque thing should actually happen, does your mumbo-jumbo tell you how to un-mumbo-jumbo again?"

"Yes, all you have to do is to repeat the process from the other end, or side, and there you are, back again."

Jones, who was urging the experiment, was a large, enthusiastic man. He had asked Mather, a smaller, more accurate colleague, to come around. He was always asking Mather around. Mather usually came, usually punctured the blister of speculation which had risen in Jones's easily inflamed mind. They generally parted with the mutual feeling of having wasted time and the mutual, if not spoken, resolve not to meet again. But they did. Perhaps, in some odd way, they needed each other. More and more those we have thought to be enemies have, at least in natural history, proved to be widely reciprocating partners; those we took to be obvious parasites and victim-hosts, closer inspection has shown to be symbiots—partners who interchange essential services.

Mather was a fairly conservative psychologist. Jones held a newly invented chair of Historical Anthropology. The crank businessman who had founded their small college had insisted that, among the standard conventional faculties, there should be this odd study. That he had chosen also to endow this professorship with one thousand dollars a year more than the endowment of any of the other chairs didn't make the position of Jones, his appointee, any easier.

But Jones was not the kind of man to care. His ebullient indifference to his conservative colleagues' envy-tinged disapproval he called "the anthropological outlook."

"We're all savages," he used to announce airily at the high table, "all, mentally, guinea pigs to be tested and studied, unless we're anthropologists." Then he would add what he called the anthropological approach: "And, of course, the anthropologist himself is only a rarer form of savage than another anthropologist, and so on ad infinitum."

"Then you have no datum of objectivity," Wilkins, the philosopher, would challenge.

"Well, there can't be—unless you could really get inside someone else."

"That wouldn't be enough," cut in Mather. "It would, to be precise, be going only halfway. To complete the process and bring it to an adequate conclusion, from the premise you have postulated, you would have not only to get inside someone else; simultaneously he would have to get inside you. Then each would have to return and compare notes."

"Yes," said Jones agreeably, "yes, that, at last, would be real experimental anthropology."

His mind floated off in speculation. The rest of the high-table discussion fell to its normal level: the food presented, the football prospects, and the local gossip.

This contribution from Mather recurred to Jones, however, a fortnight later. It and Jones's own pachydermatous good nature and eupeptic hopefulness—his digestion was never his weak spot—quite prepared him for another snub. After all, the instructions actually seemed to point to Mather.

Jones, in pursuit of his odd assignment—for his colleagues had to own that he worked as hard at his silly job and with more enthusiasm than they did at their proper ones—had been reading up on Sufi esoteric practices. One in particular had interested him. It was called "How the rainbow which circles the spray of the Fountain of Light (The Nor) may, by heart-contact, be thrown to link with another such rainbow." There followed quite unmistakable instructions as to how this rainbow interchange was to be effected.

"Well," Jones had remarked to himself as he had put the book down. "If that means anything, it means that, with quite a simple experiment, one should be able to do precisely what Mather said (and quite rightly) would alone let one have real anthropological knowledge, direct knowledge, of another person."

He went on, with growing interest, to read the further

instructions. They said that for the best or easiest results "the opposite number should be one's contrast"; if, for example, one was born under Jupiter with the sun in a neighboring "house," then one should choose as one's colleague in the experiment someone whose natal star was Saturn, with more than a glance of the Moon, or perhaps of Mercury, in his influences.

"That certainly would seem to point out Mather. His dryness would be a perfect complement to my ebullience," murmured Jones to himself, pencil in hand. "I'll try. Maybe the stars indicate our collusions as well as our collisions." Whether they do or not, the fact remains that Mather did come when called. Jones opened with a really quite good "anthropological approach."

"I've been thinking over what you said about insight into character."

"You mean that if you are to be able to see into me I must be able to the same degree to see into you?"

"Yes, that's it, and, of course, you're right."

Mather was not so desiccated that he was not a little suppled by wholehearted agreement.

"I'm glad you think so," he conceded.

So, when Jones unmasked his request, he did not immediately refuse. Jones's way of putting it, too, was not unskillful.

"I've come across a psychophysical experimental method which aims at helping such insight. Of course, I'm not a psychologist, so I can't tell if there's anything in it. I thought perhaps you'd 'vet' it for me."

"A psychophysical method of insight—do you mean an

eye exercise?" Mather was permitting himself only a very low percentage of curiosity in his question, but Jones took it as a request for more information. And once again he improved his position.

"Well, I gather it is practically nothing but a physical method—something which can be definitely tested."

That certainly reassured Mather, who was one of the almost wholly physiological psychologists.

"Well, go ahead. Describe the method."

Jones knew that this would be the turning point. He tried to preserve the favorable position he had won. But in a few minutes it was clear that he had lost heavily. He could only conclude rather feebly, "Let's try."

And then, when he thought he had failed, there came that queer little hint of interest, if only nervous interest. Jones, like many florid optimistic men, was a diabetic and had been on insulin quite a while. Little upsets like this told on him more than he chose to own to himself. His nervousness was disguised—even to himself—rather than lessened by his outward cheerfulness. He began to feel his need of the routine shot. But if Mather was going to yield, he must be pushed now. Mather fidgeted, put his hand in his pocket, pulled it out empty, and then said, "Oh, very well, let's get it over and show there's nothing in it. After all, a great deal of science still consists in pricking the bubbles of superstition!" It was hardly a gracious offer to cooperate, but Jones was ready to take it.

"The first thing is what is called the heart-contact," he said. "We have to sit as close as we can, directly opposite one another."

He drew up two stools and sat down on one. Mather methodically settled himself on the other. This was the last time, he said to his not ill-tempered but conventionally respectable self, that he would humor Jones. Even if Jones had the ear of their silly old founder, if the rest of the faculty—which was sound enough—kept steadily at sound work, the college could build up a reputation which could make it independent.

Jones interrupted this not too friendly reflection with, "Would you please draw your stool as close as possible? The point is that we have to have the left breast as close as possible to the left breast. It's to get the two hearts opposite one another."

"Two hearts that beat as one?" queried Mather crossly, but adjusting his position as asked.

Jones answered only, "Now, please draw over a little to the left"—he did so, too—"so that our faces are as much as possible face to face. And now we have to let each eye look into the eye it sees opposite it."

This, thought Mather, is worse than a bore—it's really rather unpleasant. Still, it would soon be over.

That was, as far as he could remember, his last actual reflection for a considerable time. It wasn't that he ceased to notice things. Indeed, he perceived things perhaps more clearly now than ever before. Perhaps it was that he hadn't been so interested in anything, in a sort of vivid way, since he was a child. Perhaps that was the reason he'd ceased to be able to reflect, ceased to be the detached little man with the notebook.

Jones found exactly the same thing. Perhaps he noticed it

a few seconds earlier than Mather did, since he wasn't delayed by having to get over an attack of irritation. Things had suddenly gone just as he wished, so his observations followed quite a simple route, and at a steady pace. First, he saw the bridge of his own nose reflected in Mather's eyes. It was like looking into a small, very clear, binocular camera —a sort of stereoscopic effect. He was just beginning to wonder why he had never tried this odd little experiment before, when he was disturbed by an awkward feeling—a physical feeling that he hadn't had since he'd fainted from a palpitation. His heart had begun to beat as if it were pushing itself out of his chest, and he had at the same time the sensation that this was in some way a "double event"—that Mather was suffering in the same way and that he, Jones, could directly share that unpleasantness as though it were his own. He tried to shift his attention back to his eyes and away from his chest. He was sufficiently successful, though the acute discomfort continued, to be largely distracted by what he saw.

A moment before he had been observing the bridge of his nose mirrored in the eyes which were staring into his. Now the same field of vision was before him—but not quite the same—the same details, but their order was changed. He saw his nose and, behind it, the mirror eyes—and in these what was he seeing? To clear away his confusion he lowered his focus. He saw quite clearly his own nose confronting him. He saw the broad bridge, almost a saddle, which he'd so often confronted when shaving. Squinting involuntarily, he caught sight of a high narrow bridge even closer to him.

It stuck out so far and high that he could see the white, stretched skin that covered it.

Funny, he thought, I imagined I was much too farsighted to be able to focus on anything as close as that, or, for that matter, on that nose opposite.

Suddenly, he was overcome by vertigo. What was his actual position? outlook? orientation? There wasn't any doubt. It was only fear that was making him try to question it. A blast of sheer dread struck him like a line squall. Here was real nightmare. He'd never imagined a dream as simple as this could so stun him with panic. He *must* wake up. What roused him, however, was a laugh—not a very pleasant one —but he had to own that it wasn't sinister, only ugly, and so, in a way, reassuring. Where had he heard that queer neighing cackle? Of course, it was a rather clever but quite offensive parody of his own cheerful "ha, ha."

The face close before him began to draw away. But the laughter went on; Jones could see as well as hear that now. The laughter was obviously coming from the face that was now drawn away sufficiently to be seen as a whole. There was no longer a shadow of a doubt under which to take shelter. He had to come out into the hard light of knowledge. He could see himself laughing, and that unpleasant neighing must be—if not the sound of his voice, at least what it sounded like—to whom? To Mather, of course! The mouth opposite him ceased to gape and bellow. It was about to form words. The accent of the voice was little more pleasant than its laughter.

"Well, we've done it." Jones heard the remark, a mincing parody of his own (as he'd always thought) rather clear-cut tenor. Yes, there sitting opposite him was—himself. Not quite himself, though. He knew himself, as far as appearances went, only through those daily mirror inspections when he shaved and brushed his hair. Now, of necessity, he saw himself the other way around, the right way around. It was depressing to notice the significant, if slight, differences that showed up. He had gotten used to making little compensatory disregardings of the familiar mirror presentation. For instance, he now saw that his features were not at all the symmetrical pattern he'd come to assume: one eye was distinctly lower than the other; his nose was clearly out of line; his mouth had a pouched fold on one corner and a tucked-in wrinkle in the other; the left ear stood out much further than the right. So that was the actual impression one gave. That was what one looked like when one stood outside oneself and, disembodied, looked with detachment at one's body.

The words "detachment" and "disembodied," however, running rapidly through his mind, suddenly swung him around. Of course, he wasn't detached, disembodied. There was something worse than just seeing oneself from the outside, worse than having simply dragged one's moorings: there was the actual position from which one saw that one had drifted. There was the shock of what one had run into —of being right in someone else's body. The mouth was, naturally, dry from alarm. But was that the only reason why it tasted so unpleasantly strange and stale? The tongue obeyed him as he passed it around the "tacky" gums. But in its routine efforts to freshen things up it struck against something that caught and pinched it. What was that? Of course, it must be a large upper dental plate. What a horrid thing! Thank heaven, he had kept his own teeth—all but a little bridgework—"the bridge of sighs," he called it jokingly to himself, for sometimes he could hear his breath whistle through it. But, of course, that was just what he hadn't done. He'd lost his own carefully tended body and was now shut up in this dilapidated makeshift. He swallowed with fear—fear of having to make an inventory that might disclose heaven-knew-what lapses, lesions, and disgusts. The swallow was not a success. Hell! had one to learn how someone else does everything? He began to cough. Swollen tonsils had given him that choke. Mather had evidently never taken proper care of his body. He began to sneeze. The nose was apparently as neglected as the throat. He snatched for a handkerchief. It was certainly in keeping with all the rest. But there was no choice.

Shaken by the sneezing, that confounded huge dental plate nearly flew out of his mouth. He was so disgustedly vexed that he almost let it slip out. He felt he wanted to stamp on it to express his revulsion. The thought that there was someone to protest against brought him to his outer senses again. Yes, there he was—his real self, sitting in front of him. He could no longer see his old body—dear, delightful, most precious of all objects—clearly, for it had retreated. The stool on which it was still seated was now pushed back still farther. Of course, he couldn't see as clearly as he was used to seeing. He remembered that Mather, like most petti-fogging, hairsplitting, overaccurate persons, was nearsighted. His own body, it was clear, however, wasn't being pushed about yet. That was a relief. Mather—after that first explosion of startled humor—must have been even more stunned than he was by what had happened.

Well, he, Jones, must pull himself together—or, rather, this old rag bag Mather had left to him. He must hurry. For he suddenly realized that Mather must be told how to take care of the Jones body. He might, by some sudden, careless, foolish action, strain or break part of that body—clumsy little ass.

Jones got to his feet—but not very skillfully. As he discovered when he tried to bend it quickly, the left knee was stiff, indeed, quite arthritic, and judging by the feel, there were some quite savage corns on the right toes. But the body was lighter and he was nearer the floor when he stood up. Of course, Mather was a smaller man by some inches. He stepped over to where his own body was seated. It looked up at him with a queer, stiff twist of the neck.

"Shall I give you a hand up?" Jones-in-Mather asked Mather-in-Jones.

"No," came that queer voice in reply. "It's a damned clumsy overgrown thing you've swapped on me. But I'd better learn to ride it myself."

"Well, it's better than being cramped up as I am!"

"Don't make personal remarks," the other one snapped. "This body seems pretty well out of condition."

"You take care of it," exclaimed Jones. "You're very careless, I'm finding out, about how to take care of a body. And that body you're in, just because it is a fine one, needs care."

"Oh, damn you," began Mather. Then they both broke into feeble laughter.

"Well," Jones remarked finally, "we've got a double hold

on each other, there's no doubt. We'd better each set about quietly finding out how to run these machines."

They were silent for some time, as each returned to his internal inventory. While doing this Jones, though, watched Mather. He saw Mather move the Jones hand up to the Jones face and feel and pat it gingerly. Why should he do that? There was nothing to be ashamed of or disgusted at in that fine ruddy cheek. Suddenly the Jones voice addressed him: "You take care of that plate. You haven't got one. Don't you lose it."

Jones felt he must retaliate for this insult, the gross insult of being told to take care—as though it were precious—of a contraption which was a disgusting injury to have stuffed in one's mouth. He was seized with a craving to spit the beastly thing out. Wiser second thoughts prevailed. He contended himself with retaliating: "You take care of that left eye. Those eyes see twice as far as yours do, but the left one needs care—don't go straining it."

"It's half-blind," said Mather, turning the Jones-head down, raising the Jones-wrist, and looking at the wrist watch. "I can hardly see the watch hands!"

"You've never been able to see across the room. Look at those books in the bookcase over there."

Jones saw Mather turn the Jones-head toward the books and become interested.

"Yes," came the grudging acknowledgment. "It's queer to see as far as that with the naked eye."

"And now look out of the window."

Mather ambled the big Jones-body across the room.

"I feel a bit as though I were on stilts," he giggled as he

passed his own body. Then, at the window, he added: "It is rather fun with these long-distance eyes of yours. Spectacles don't quite give all that."

For a few minutes they walked about, each trying out his borrowed surface senses. Jones was quite amused to see what amazing detail he could now see on the dial of his watch. Then he scanned the back of the hairy Mather-hand that had risen up and held itself in front of these new, shortly keen eyes which were now his, as though that hand had obeyed him all his life.

Next, he turned to trying out the ears. They were certainly different—not any sharper, he thought, but more inclined to relish sound just for itself. He remembered that Mather, of course, played the piano. He wondered what it would be like to play? Would one really have to care for music? Or would the fingers simply run away of themselves, up and down the keyboard, as quickly and as mechanically as one of those old Pianolas?

His interior investigations were disturbed by hearing his former body speak. Mather was complaining in that voice which he, Jones, was still certain that Mather was putting on to make him hear how ridiculous he sounded. Mather, too, was quiggling, in a ridiculous way, his borrowed hands.

"Why, they're nearly paralyzed," he squeaked.

"Don't be insulting."

"Well, don't make my voice sound so absurd. You've been doing that to insult me!" answered Mather.

So, Jones reflected, we sound equally ridiculous to each other. This mollified him considerably and he replied soothingly: "It's because you can play and I can't. It's amusing, this end, to feel a hand as live as that."

Mather, too, was soothed, and a new sensation distracted Jones: something sharp that shot right up the inner side of his leg. He twisted the leg again, and again that pain shot, keen as toothache. Heavens, he thought, so that's sciatica.

The two figures walked up and down the big open study. An onlooker would have thought they were two philosophers lost in reflection over some shared intellectual problem. In truth, they were both engrossed in nothing but feeling. Each was wandering up and down the strange lodging in which he found himself; trying the doors, the odd cupboards, the back rooms; looking down mysterious ill-lit passages; listening in at private telephones; peering out from mysterious windows. It was like moving through a strange house at dusk and every now and then tripping over wires which gave you a shock, switched on a light, or rang a bell.

After a silence, Jones heard Mather muttering again in that provoking Jones-parody voice:

"It's a clumsy body," the voice said.

"Nonsense," he retorted. "It's simply because you don't know how to run a high-powered car. Don't you go flinging it about. It's a bigger thing than you're used to."

"Well, you take care of mine. You're not used to as fine a piece of mechanism."

A sudden gust of anger swept through Jones. He felt a strong temptation to pinch one of these highly prized fingers in the door—only then he, Jones, would have to endure all the pain.

Well, it was no use wrangling. Mather was so stupid as

only to be vexed by this predicament, but he, Jones, should surely be interested in such a brilliant success. He was determined that he would be—though perhaps it was rather more of an adventure than he had been able to foresee. But, before going any further, there was a lot of interest to be gained from learning at firsthand—and indeed more than first*hand*—about another body's little ways. This was real exploration; going further, after all, than any human exploration had ever gone. And, once you got over your disgust, the actual way of exploring was rather fun. It was a little like being out on the road for the first time on a sort of mysterious bicycle which completely enclosed you, but which you had to balance and drive every moment. The machine gave queer little swoops and dives. In another way it was like being moved into a new house with a new set of servants. The things one used to require were still supplied, but were never to be found in quite the same places the old staff in the old house used to put them. This Matherbody had a number of odd tricks. For instance, you had to know when it really wanted to sneeze and play other pneumatic tricks, and when it was only shamming—or, at least, not intending to go through with the thing. You'd get all ready, standing by with a pocket handkerchief out, and, then, on the brink, the body would change its mind.

Suddenly, as Jones was congratulating himself on how well he was tumbling to its ways and getting its drift, it put up a new problem to him. It was a sort of itch, or perhaps craving would be a better word. Did it want food? No; there was certainly the remains of a meal in its stomach. A drink? No; the throat wasn't wanting liquid; that was clear. And yet the throat or mouth was wanting something. Jones was so puzzled that he glanced over to the Mather-possessed body. He saw Mather pull up the Jones-hand and put it into the pocket of the Jones-coat. Now, that was going too far! Swap bodies, maybe, but you must respect personal property. Next, Mather would be reading his private correspondence. In a sort of retaliation, Jones stuck one of the queer effeminate hands—which were all he had now to rely on—into Mather's pocket. It surprised him. It was hardly in before it closed on something and drew it out. A pipe! Of course, Mather smoked and he, Jones, did not. That queer craving must be for tobacco. He looked across and saw that his body had ceased to rummage in his pockets. Again there came that parody-laugh to which he couldn't get used.

"Of course," Mather was saying to him, "of course, it's my body that wants to smoke, though, for a moment, I was absent-mindedly rummaging for my pipe, as I knew it was time for one."

By that time Jones had found that his borrowed, burrowing fingers had lit on a tobacco pouch.

"You'd better have a smoke for me," cackled the parody-voice. "Then I'll not be feeling nicotine starved when I get back."

Fancy, thought Jones, having to stoke this beastly little body in this filthy way just to keep it comfortable for its tobacco-addicted owner.

But the demand was in him now. It was he who now felt the wish to smoke. But how? He'd never smoked in his life; had always hated the silly, dirty habit. His own body drew across to him and, through it, Mather said, "Here, give me the pipe and pouch." But after some fumbling Mather exclaimed:

"Damn these chilblained fingers! They can't even pack a pipe."

Jones had begun to want so much to smoke that he swallowed the insult. Together, they managed to get the pipe filled.

"Now, don't burn my suit or my fingers," was Mather's last provoking advice. But as soon as he was sucking at the pipe a sense of ease and tolerance rose up in Jones's mind. He felt it was ridiculous, but there it was and, as it was pleasant, why not yield to it? Jones sat down. At least, until this pipe was finished, there was no need to do anything else. After all, it was the only pipe he would ever enjoy in his life. He knew, once back in his proper body, he would hate the beastly thing. He stretched himself back in a chair and noticed idly that, as he himself had become relaxed, Mather, in the Jones body, seemed to be becoming proportionately restless. After fidgeting about increasingly, he turned at last on Jones.

"Jones," he called, "is there anything wrong with this body of yours? I'm beginning to feel queer, devilish queer. You didn't eat something at lunch which disagreed with you, and then slip out and sit smoking comfortably in my body while I have to do the digesting?"

He was obviously in angry distress which was evidently growing, so Jones hastened to reassure him, at least on that count.

"No, no," he answered in quite a placatory tone—or, at least, in one that was as mollifying as he could make Mather's sharp little voice manage: "No, I assure you I didn't. Never do. I eat very sparingly. In fact, I'm on a moderate diet."

As he said that, the thought, the explanation, flashed into his mind. Lord! How forgetful one becomes away from home! He put down the pipe he was now holding quite expertly and rose in real concern. He fumbled, found Mather's watch, and looked at it. Yes, it was true enough: it was full time—a bit over, in point of fact. He went over to his Mather-occupied body or, rather, the body that was now wholly occupying—engrossing Mather.

"It'll be all right in a minute. I'll show you what to do."

Mather only looked at him with dumb distress in his Jones-eyes. Then the mouth muttered weakly: "Can't you get me out of this?" He was too tired, evidently, even to protest.

"Yes, yes," said Jones reassuringly. "In a moment, in just a moment we'll change back. But just now—" He paused. The truth was that he was frightened, too—more frightened, maybe, than Mather was. For Mather didn't know what was wrong with him: what was giving out under him. Jones did. He didn't dare risk the change-over—with all that almost suffocating acceleration of the heart—when his body, with Mather inside it, might collapse before he was back in it and able to do what he knew must be done. What a fool he'd been not to keep an eye on the time. Of course, being out of his body he wouldn't have the warning sensation and, equally of course, Mather wouldn't know what those first symptoms would be signaling.

Well, somehow he must face Mather and get him to do what had to be done. Otherwise there were only two other facts to be faced. Which of them would be the worse, he couldn't imagine. One was Mather's dying of the body Mather was now in, falling down and falling to pieces, and Mather's going—going, literally, only heaven knew where—and he, Jones, living, spending the rest of his life in this absurd little spidery body—already more than half a dozen years older than he was; and—horrors!—having to take up life in Mather's house—in Mather's body, it would be the only place he would be allowed to live. To have to share the house with wizened, frisky little Mrs. Mather—he who was unmarried and a misogynist—and those awful, noisy, impudent, dirty children. . . .

There was, of course, the one other choice: to be certified as a lunatic by maintaining the truth: that he was Jones in Mather's body and that Mather had died in Jones's.

The thought roused him to desperation. He seized his own body by the arm. How odd to feel one's body from the outside! But there was no more time for such reflections.

"Come," he said hurriedly. "Lean on me if you feel you're going to faint."

Somehow he got that huge, heeling bulk across the passage and up the three stairs into the bathroom. He snatched the hypodermic from the small mirror cabinet. He slumped the Jones body down on the seat, then propped it up and set about loading the syringe. But, heavens!, these neat little hands, which could deftly fill a pipe and run freely enough on the piano keyboard, now fumbled almost as though they were frostbitten. Once, he nearly dropped the little glass tube of the cylinder on the floor tiles. Then his inept fingers pulled the plunger out too far, and it came clean away from the tube. But at last, by dint of sheer schooling, he got those incompetent hands to carry the loaded instrument at the ready. He pushed back the sleeve on his old body's forearm. Mather was roused by this.

"What the devil are you doing?" he whispered in helpless anger.

"You'll be all right in a moment," replied Jones. But would he? Anyhow, it was clear that a moment or two would decide, one way or the other, and, probably, for good. He pinched up the skin of the left forearm. He'd so often, quickly and deftly, plucked up the flesh on his leg in that way. But these wretched Mather-fingers fell down on that, too. At last he had a good fold fairly well held with the left hand. He brought the needle near with his right. Of course, it caught badly in the skin—wouldn't make a good piercing. He pressed the plunger feebly. The liquid began to ooze out over the skin. He jabbed savagely. Mather stirred in the collapsed body and just succeeded in making it say, "So, you're finishing me off with a shot of poison. That's why . . ." His voice trailed away.

But the needle had gone in with a tear—right in—too deep, really, but what did he care?—it was in. That was all that mattered now. He drove the plunger home and saw the skin swell above the buried slant of the hollow needle. He whipped it out, stuck a patch of cotton on the puncture, and waited, bent over the body—his body, which he must bring back. Gradually it stirred, though the eyes were now closed. He shuffled the hypodermic behind the bathroom seat. Yes, the body was coming alive. So great was his relief that he dragged the hulk on his shoulder, drew it out of the bathroom back into the sitting room, and plumped it into a chair. As the body sank back, he heard Mather saying in a vague, accentless voice, "What went wrong? What's wrong with this damned body anyway?"

Jones's mind was working quickly now. He dragged a stool forward to the right side of the chair in which his body sat, held up by the chair's straight back. He pushed himself forward in Mather's body, until the two bodies were left-breast to left-breast. He could actually feel the dull labored thump of the Jones heart like a slow bass scored under the hard, thick stroke of the Mather-heart, which had had some pretty stiff pumping to do in the last ten minutes. He swung the Mather-face close to his old face. The lids were still lowered.

"Mather!" he said. "Look at me!"

The eyes opened and gazed steadily, absent-mindedly, as a baby will stare when absorbed in taking its bottle. That would do. Jones gazed out through the very short-ranged Mather-eyes into the two pupils opposite him. He felt his heart begin to quieten: slower and slower it beat. He felt relaxed and easy. Then he felt his heart rise in its beats again—not distressingly but with a series of rapid, strong strokes. And then, once again, it began to smooth out its emphasis and become as steady as before. He rested back comfortably. The face opposite him drew away. He was able to look past it and idly read the titles on the book backs across the room.

Suddenly Mather's voice broke on his ear: "It's not a safe method. But I own it's the quickest I've ever come across for hypnosis."

Jones sat up.

"It put you under deeper than it put me. You're hardly around yet," Mather's voice continued, "but one would expect that. A trained psychologist is always the most difficult of all people to put under."

Jones got to his feet. Yes, they were his own familiar, comfortable, cornless feet. "Well," he remarked, "thank you for trying it out with me."

"Oh, nothing, nothing," said Mather airily. "But, take my advice, and leave such experimenting to trained psychologists. I don't mind telling you that you're looking pretty queer." He paused. Then he went on, with a note of grudging curiosity coming into his voice: "I may as well tell you that when I was a student I was hypnotized a number of times, for experimental purposes. But I don't remember ever having had any dreams at all like those I had during our little experiment. Did you have any queer fancies?"

Jones gave a noncommittal grunt. Mather stood for a moment, uncertain whether or not to probe further. Finally he said to himself, It must have been the Freudian "transference" working in dream-imagery form. But, I must say, I never expected the feeling-provoked fantasy could be so convincing. It is certainly not safe. Certainly not.

He walked to the door. "Well, good-by; and you'll take my advice, won't you? No more experimenting of this sort." Jones shook hands with him and got rid of him with another series of thanks.

When he returned from letting the little man out, he stood for a moment, still and silent in the middle of the room. Then he remarked to himself in a soft voice: "Maybe he is right.

Really, it could only have been a dream." But, after another moment, he turned, went out of the room, through the passage, and into the bathroom. He bent down. Behind the bathroom seat lay the hypodermic syringe. He pulled up his left sleeve. On the lower forearm was a big, clumsy puncture with a small scrap of reddened cotton still adhering to it. He looked at his watch.

"Well," he muttered, "if it *was* a dream, it not only took its time about it, but it troubled to produce quite a lot of circumstantial evidence. It was certainly a dream that cared enough for verisimilitude to dress the part. It was a dream with such a sense of the dramatic that it first nearly pushed me right out of the basic dream of this life, but, having taken me to the brink, it swung me back again. I've never heard of a patient who overslept the time of his injection long enough to bring himself to the verge of collapse and then, in his dream, not only sleepwalked and gave himself the dose in the nick of time, but who also troubled to invent another character, taken from one of his colleagues. And this character is brought in not only to give him the dose but, with a novelist's love for accuracy of character, the colleague is made to give the injection so damn badly that the dreamer deals himself a sore arm for two weeks! Anyhow, that's what I'm in for!"

He paused and then went on to himself. "But it'll be more than two weeks before I'll be able to decide if that was a dream or really a switch-over for a while. If it really was, if one actually saw from the other side, well, then it was worth the discomfort and the risk. But there's the rub: one never *will* be quite sure—at least, till one has gone to the other side for good—and then it'll be too late to make a report of the sort that any of my colleagues would even listen to. However, I suppose Mather is right: whether it was hypnosis or a real transference, one shouldn't try it again. But if only I wasn't a diabetic, I think I'd have another try!"

DROMENON

The origin of religion is in something done. Around that doing, that process, that performed pattern, there grows up the structure so outlined. Religion is a dromenon, a pattern of dynamic expression in which the performers express something larger than themselves, beyond their powers of speech to express and a therapeutic rhythm in which they find release and fulfillment.

Jane Harrison ANCIENT ART AND RITUAL

Civilized man thinks out his difficulties, at least, he thinks he does. Primitive man dances out his difficulties.

Dr. R. R. Marrett ANTHROPOLOGY

Preface by Mark Jocelyn, F.S.A.

SYLVESTER SHELBOURNE'S SUDDEN death has laid on me a very great responsibility. As his literary executor I had expected I should have had to undertake considerable labor, labor which I had naturally hoped would be postponed for many years. But, now, not only has it come upon me prematurely; unexpectedly it has presented me with a problem even more unexpected, even more painful. The shock which I have experienced is the more severe for two reasons: in the first place, I saw him but a week before his death. I was struck, and not only with his apparent health. Always a vital man, I was so impressed with his vitality that day as to remark on it to him, saying that I hoped it presaged the completion of his great work. He replied, with quiet assurance, that he believed it did. That could only mean for me, or for any who knew him, that he was ready to issue his magnum opus, on *The Essential Ideas of Gothic Architecture,* a subject in which he deserved the title of a triumphant revolutionary and wherein, as all scholars know, he had brought his studies to the point at which even his most stubborn critics had to own his proofs were nearly clinched.

We spoke of a visit which he had lately made to reinvestigate some outlying and neglected evidence, and, though he went into no particulars, I left with the assurance that his great work was achieved. Alas: his work was over, but in another sense than I had dreamed. Nor can I have the melancholy satisfaction of knowing that he closed his case with his life. Thence sprang the second shock I have sustained. I turned to my sad task sustained by the thought that I should, at least, be permitted to present to the world the triumphant vindication of my honored friend's lifework. I found, instead of a final series of proofs, needing only to be assembled—a narrative, a narrative of an experience so strange that, had I not known of his sanity from having visited him after the event he records and only a few days before he made his record, I would have been impelled to suspect mental derangement.

I have suffered greatly in my effort to decide what was best to be done. Finally I have resolved to obey the letter of my charge. As his literary executor I am not permitted to suppress documents which the testator considered of vital importance. I do not believe that he was insane. In these circumstances, painful though it is to me—very jealous as I am of our science's prestige in general, and of his reputation in particular—I believe I have no choice. Publish I must. My one comfort lies in the fact, often illustrated in the past in antiquarian studies, that evidence, preserved in the face of ridicule and dismay has not infrequently (after those who bore the obloquy of bearing such undesired witness have died in ignorance of their service) given rise to new inquiries which have revolutionized the science which they served.

It only remains for me to complete my evidence by saying that Sylvester Shelbourne was found, seated at his desk, with the actual manuscript—the text of which follows—before him; the final page uppermost, his pen laid beside: he had evidently died as he read the last page through. Medical and legal inspection succeeded only in disclosing one other fact of any possible significance. The body was found in perfect condition. There was no known cause of death. The fact concerned his surroundings. On his desk there had always stood, on a small ebony plinth, a large crystal ball some four inches in diameter. It was gone. Instead, the desk was covered with a fine dust made of minute quartz fragments. Careful inspection showed, however, that none of these had entered the mouth or nasal passages.

Journal and Memorandum of my last Examination of the Cathedral and Collegiate Church of St. Aidans.

St. Aidans is little visited by tourists for three reasons. Firstly, it is out of the way. Secondly, it lacks any richness of decoration—a large collegiate church out on the Celtic marshes naturally suffered a "denudation" and "dereliction" more thorough and prolonged than did those nearer the Continent and the Counter Reformation. Thirdly and finally, it suffered last of the cathedrals. Restoration, as we know, went through three stages: a first stage of agreed iconoclasm in the name of a wholly inadequate knowledge; a second, of agreed preservation in the name of scholarly agnosticism; and a third stage, when all agreement vanished and every chapter did what was right in its own eyes. St. Aidans felt the full force of this final attack. A rich brewer gave the money; a dictatorial dean the impetus. With St. Aidans the synoptic warning was reversed: to him that hath nothing, to him shall be given even that which he never could have had.

Gregorian was Dean Bathurst's delight. As an undergraduate he had watched with the enthusiasm of a Josiah the great nineteenth-century vaudeville organs torn out like lying tongues from the cathedrals and installed in their stead those demure instruments on which Bach's polyphony may be rendered. But when he became a Canon, Gregorian chanting, the ineffectual hope of the Tractarians, made another assault from its great fortress of Solesmes. Its new champions declared its first failure as an ecclesiastical comeback in Britain was due to inadequate rendering. No one who, during the nineteenth century, heard a High Church attempting plain song, could doubt the failure.

Its new champions, among whom Dean Bathurst was a stalwart, allowed that this was so. They maintained, however, that if only the right accompaniment could be found, then we should understand why plain song was the voice of real devotion, and how it had held for two thousand and more years (the enthusiasts claimed not only David but Tubal-cain among the virtuosos of their art) the ear of mankind. All this, as every antiquarian knows, might well have remained speculation freaked with unconvincing experiment, but for the discovery of St. Guthlac's psalter. I need not recall the interest that find awoke: The oddness of the discovery itself—that in the binding of seven consecutive (and never-read) moldering volumes of Archbishop Usher's sermons (and, as they were actually moldering, I will not recall the Cathedral Library in which they were salvaged) should have been found sheet after sheet of the invaluable late Saxon manuscript.

Delicate research with ultraviolet lenses revealed that, charming as was the addition to our still far-from-complete series of great scriptory work, a greater treasure was concealed under the surface, as beneath the beautiful surface of a scenic lake may lie sunken treasure. The unique discovery was that the final page (on which now appear those knots and interlacements which scholarship—my own among them—dismissed as late attempts to imitate the full fancy of the Celtic frets from the Durrow and Kells manuscripts) that page disclosed, underneath what then seemed to us pointless decoration (now I know better) an actual scale drawing. Someone had taken the trouble, in an idle afternoon, to make a working plan of an Anglo-Saxon organ!

Of course, all scholars and semischolars had long known of the descriptions of those strange instruments given in the Anglo-Saxon chronicle—the two respectively at Winchester and Peterborough being credited with psychophysical powers, with a volume of literally heart-shaking and blood-beating sound, which has made all later readers smile. But again I must note that though I once joined in that superior humor, I do so no longer.

The find remained, for nearly everyone, simply a literary windfall, an unsuspected illustration to history. But one man decided to act on it: Dean Bathurst. He would have an organ actually made, a life-size model from the manuscript description, and he would install it in gaunt St. Aidans as the proper vehicle for the Gregorian chant.

Like the rest of my antiquarian colleagues, I treated this as the last extravagance of restoration. We boycotted the plan. Bathurst the Barbarian, the Dean was dubbed. One or two semicomic accounts appeared in the popular press, describing the sound the new organ gave. We were willing to believe it was as grotesque as the ignorant reporters said. Nevertheless, the very desolation of St. Aidans ("with the abomination standing where it should not," said one of my clerical fellow scholars as we discussed it)—the very fact that the ordinary expert believed there was nothing aboveground to attract an intelligent sightseer, made my visit necessary. I say at once that to admit it more than repaid the effort is an utterly inadequate phrase, though that effort was far greater than any archaeological expedition I have ever taken. I never paid a visit to any—shrine (yes, I use the hackneyed word advisedly, precisely) which gave me any experience approaching what I found in that worn hull of stone. Why, then, have I not revisited it? It is partly to explain that fact that I have written this. For the questioner is right if he supposes that I did find there the final clue to my studies, and, more, far more—a solution, I believe, to the whole psychological mystery of Gothic.

As those will know who have followed my *Further Studies in the Lancet Style,* I had come to the conclusion that we should never understand the inner significance and germinal urge of that architectural form by looking at the elevations. Interesting though they may be in themselves, they are (as I believe I have shown in my last essay, and this I take to be my chief discovery) only symptoms, resultants from the plan. I can say I knew that "Gothic" is simply the marking out and covering over of certain paths, certain, as a Greek would say, *dromena*—ways of rhythm. In the sanctuary, there is the intense nuclear pattern; around it, in the ambulatory and the great processional aisles, is the outer wave of more evident movement. I knew that, and yet I really knew about it only as a man who discovered a fossilized white anthill might make a map of it and think he could, from that, understand the termite instincts.

I arrived at St. Aidans on an autumn day. The journey is a tiring one—cross-country—with long junction waits, and the small town is the single line's terminus. I had risen early that morning, to arrive in time for evensong and, if possible, to get in a few studies and measurements before the service began, after which the cathedral would be locked up for the night. I did not want to ask any favor of the Dean; indeed, I understood he had resented the learned boycott so much that he might well have refused it. I would enter as a stranger within his gates. The whole visit opened with becoming drabness. In a last dribble of market-town passengers, I went down the small platform, past the tired little engine which had come to its daily standstill, confronting with its buffers those terminus buffers which always have the look of termination without finality. "This is the end," they seem to indicate, "not because it is the goal, but because there's just nothing beyond worth going further for." Even Ulysses, I reflected, would have turned back here, as at the barrier I gave up the outward half of my return ticket. I remember actually feeling a queer gleam of relief that I had a return. Think what it would mean if, instead of being an elderly man of active leisure, I had been a poor young tutor coming down here to be buried alive in this dismal little country corner "where all things are forgotten"—even the few that have ever been known.

Certainly, coming out from the train hutch in which we had been detrained, one felt all one's forebodings had been fulfilled. The day was one of those dismal western days which attain to a neutrality that is positively dreadful. The light was gray, shed or, rather, exuded from a sky which gave no shadows. And this perfectly dull illumination showed a scene that certainly deserved no better rendering—an area wide but not spacious had around its edge houses of weathered stucco, or gray-yellow stockbrick and one or two of a stone which managed to look as though it were a blend of the dismal brick and the dreary plaster. I took this inventory as I trudged across the "Railway Square," which a rusty cast-iron plate fastened to a lamppost informed me the area had been christened, no doubt, in the fifties. My eye, like the dove out of the ark, looked across the inundation of ugliness, seeking some small space, some Georgian façade, on which it might rest. "No," as the poem on suicide says, "No, there was none." The only thing was to lift up one's eyes to one's goal. Yes, there it was and, in its way, as daunting as the town. St. Aidans may have had a tower but, if so, it had certainly been built of the local sandstone and had certainly collapsed. Bishop Creighton's witticism came into my mind: "As the verger says 'Some of the chancel bays are twelfth-century,' the intelligent reply-question is, 'When did the central tower fall?' "

Over the meaner roofs of the town rose the long leaden roof of the nave, like the back of a stranded whale. I left my bag at an inn which, like a hermit crab, had worked its way into part of the decayed cloister buildings and, from that coign, had put out its claws to catch the passing visitor. Once inside the cathedral, I experienced some relief; if not inviting, at least it was not as forbidding as the gaunt exterior. Further, I was allowed to make my measurements without interference. I was needing some allover circumferential reckonings, so that I did not enter the chancel itself. And the ambulatories—certainly one of the good modern innovations—were unguarded by that blind leader of the blind—the sixpenny-collecting verger guide. Indeed, I saw no one about—I supposed the verger was in the choir vestries getting ready for evensong—at least no official was on sentry go. Once or twice I thought I saw another visitor. Fortunately he seemed as busy as I with his own observations of the place. I own it did once enter my mind to speculate who he could be: Someone, evidently, investigating with scholarly care a cathedral which all normal scholars had long dismissed as hopeless? If he were a casual ignoramus, then why this careful scrutiny? If he were really as learned—yes, I had better be honest and record my full semiconscious vanity—as I, then why didn't I know him? I knew no one in Britain was as far advanced as I in this investigation. My theories were tolerated among the F.S.A. simply because my detailed knowledge was greatest—that is not vanity but fact. They would never have given me the hearing I had won unless my factual information had surpassed theirs. There were only two men who might possibly be on this clue—François Peliot and Karl Heiser. But I knew both of them by sight, and this man, though I only caught sight of him every now and then moving in the distance, was quite unlike Heiser's globular body or Peliot's little lobster-like form. He was certainly tall and free-moving. I recalled a doctor once showing me that it was really easier to judge a mental state by looking at a man in the distance than close up—carriage told so much about the attitude of mind. Indeed, I became vexed with myself at my lack of attention to the subject I had in hand.

I settled down to double-check on my measurements and their correlates, and they were interesting and satisfying enough to keep me so engrossed that, with a start, I realized the cathedral had come to life.

A bell was tolling—the chancel gates stood open—candles

were alight in the sanctuary, and in the stalls there was a stir of feet, the sharp edges of the original sounds furred in the innumerable echoes. But under all these familiar sounds of an oncoming office was something else, quite unrecognizable—a sigh, but a sigh with a strange impetus in it. At times it most nearly resembled the sound which might be given by a huge aeolian harp, but at others the quality changed, and the note was like what I had once heard when an anthropologist from Australia had demonstrated for us the aborigine's siren, the "bull-roarer." Then it took on again the strange volume I once heard pour from the twenty-foot-long Tibetan lama trumpet and finally it rose to a tone I have only heard once before, when a paleontologist blew into one of those paleolithic ocarinas—certainly man's oldest wind instrument. The sounds had been so unexpected that, until they ceased, I had not asked myself whence they could be coming, what could be emitting them. Then, of course, I realized—it must be the reconstructed Saxon organ.

After that I was resolved to stay to evensong and presented myself for admission at the choir gates. I was the only applicant, the only "congregation," so I was promoted to one of the richly carved stalls on the north side. I was pleased at this, for it gave me a good coign from which to see the organ, which now had thoroughly aroused my interest. I own that for a moment I glanced about, wondering whether anyone else beside the choir and dignitaries would attend, and I remember casually wondering what had happened to my fellow investigator of the nave, wondering why he had not had the courtesy (which I own I had nearly omitted) to attend service after sight-seeing. My speculations were, however, suddenly answered, for when I turned my attention to what I had entered the choir to see and hear—the new organ—I could not doubt, though the figure was seen from the back, and the seat at the organ console was low and curtained, that there was the visitor whose tracks had crossed mine that afternoon. I was a little amused at my mistake of taking as more of an outsider than myself a chief official of the cathedral—but beyond that, and a casual wonder why a musician who must know the building, if anything, too well, and spend too much compulsory time in it, should spend a free early afternoon looking at it —I gave my attention to the instrument rather than the executant. Not that he was not remarkable. I could see that anyone who could so handle so strange a machine must be remarkably gifted. But at that moment the choir began to enter, the black-and-white "crocodile" composed of the usual complement of boys and men, with two vicars choral. A couple of full canons, like king penguins, waddled behind guided by their vergers, who dully penned or nested them, drew red curtains around them, and the service began.

Dean Bathurst, I was glad to see, was absent for the day. The responses did not reveal much. I could judge that the choir was well trained, and also suspected that there were some fine voices in it, but that I knew was to be expected —the further you go away from plastic beauty in the British Isles, the nearer you come to beauty of tone. The Celt was a master of sound, not of sight—the Welsh are natural singers, and singularly indifferent to beauty of form. The Psalms, however, were a revelation: it was not merely that the pointing was perfect. The strange instrument, with its unsuspected intervals, built up behind the chanted words a sense of volume which gave the words themselves a background that made one realize that one was listening to lamentations and exultations, despairs and aspirations, that were not merely old when Nineveh was new, but were dateless. The little human cry seemed to be breaking like a surface crest from a deep billow of universal desire and bafflement. The great breathing of the instrument rose and fell behind the voices. The only simile that I can think of which will at all describe the three-dimensional richness—the feeling that this music was, as it were, extending down time as well as filling space—is a crude one, I know. There are some frets which are pretty enough in themselves, but, place one behind the other, and there a sudden unsuspected richness of pattern is revealed.

The Magnificat and the Nunc Dimittis were really quite splendid—but stranger. The chants for the Psalter had been clear and consistent plain song, which owed its arresting quality to the fine and careful singing being backed and unbelievably enriched by the outstanding handling of this unique instrument. With the two Christian chorales I could not help feeling—though, as it will be seen, I am no musician—that some local composer—perhaps the odd organist—had developed a new composition. I had often been told that Bach's extraordinary achievement was due to the fact that he resolutely continued to develop polyphony when the more superficial masters were certain it was wholly worked out and hurried on to the newer lodes. It crossed my mind that in the music I was hearing some new "old master" was being even more radically conservative—he was going back to an even earlier mode and from an earlier level of music's development was restarting its progress. The way we have gone may seem to us inevitable, and even the best, but he is indeed provincial who believes the particular progress we have followed to be the only one. The anthem was even more remarkable. The libretto was St. Francis' famous hymn to the sun. I can only say that the music was certainly equal to those words, which have now about them an overtone of inspiration.

I was glad of the pause which the final prayers gave for recollection. But as the choir withdrew, another voluntary—the equal of that which had first surprised me—flowed out again. When it stopped I thought hours must have passed but, looking up, I saw the light was yet good—indeed, better, for the sun, as it westered, had evidently found apertures in the gray sky, and now, as I glanced up through the bare windows of the choir clerestory, I could see that it was sending its beams the length of the building. I also noticed with the same glance that in the upper trefoiling of the windows' traceries there still remained small fragments of the original stained glass. It was possible that the verger might not close the place until sundown, at least if he saw that someone was still seriously sight-seeing. I glanced down for a moment to see whether the organist were still *in situ.* Shouldn't I tell him what uncommon pleasure his playing had given me and inquire what composer's work he had been performing? But I hesitated. Experts, I had to own, are not always gracious toward ignorant admirers. Should I be risking a snub?

While I questioned, the light in the organist's small curtained bay went out, and the dim figure disappeared—he could evidently leave the choir from some small entrance by the console. Well, fate had decided. I was to stick to my last and leave amateur admiration alone. I went into the nave and certainly soon felt I was rewarded for my choice. The trefoiling of the clerestory contained a neat but not too difficult set of clues to the history of the building. There was the rebus of Abbot Blessington—a hand with two fingers raised, stuck out of a barrel or tun—Abbot Blessington, who had reared this gaunt clerestory. There, in another bay, were the white branching deer's horns with a little crucifix set in them. A window to St. Eustace had probably stood beneath, but the reference, no doubt, dated the window, for unhappy Edward II himself was said to have seen the silver stag of Cranborne Chase, a fact which first was taken as proving his oncoming doom but which, when his son had won the throne, supported the popular claim that he had been more than one-half a martyr.

Next, I was delighted to find a pure piece of medallion glass, glass, of course, much earlier than its actual fourteenth-century setting, a lovely little translucent mosaic of jeweled lumps of pure "pot metal," set like an early Limoges enamel in a thick coiling of lead. There must have been some particular reason to induce Abbot Blessington—for I assume it must have been done under his orders—to salvage this medallion or, rather, three hearts of medallions (for the three topmost cusps of the window each carried a knot of this early glasswork). The color was fine but, of course, the whole style would have seemed to a fourteenth-century builder as old-fashioned and clumsy as Jacobean furniture seemed to Christopher Wren. No, it wasn't beauty which had saved these old hearts of a departed glory. But, if not beauty, then it must have been sense, significance? Anyhow, who, without the strong glasses I carried, could have enjoyed this minute jewelry?

That second question was the last I could frame, and it closed the inquiry, for all my antiquarianism gave me no clue. I ventured a random guess to myself that the right and left coils might be some form of notation, perhaps musical notation. I tried to satisfy my daunted scholar's pride by fancying that the center one might have been a mosaic design for a face, made—as sometimes twelfth- and thirteenth-century glassmakers did—of so many small pieces—tesserae, they may almost be called—that some slipped out from the clasp of the soft lead when the window glass was shifted, and that these fragments had been hoisted again and reframed.

It was while I had become absorbed in this little, and literally out-of-the-way, riddle, that I became aware that I was—not being followed, but accompanied. The thought, "It's the verger, wanting to close and yet afraid to speak," was about as faint as the visual impression from the corner of my binocular-visored eye. I shifted a little, toward the west end and the great tower arch which terminated the nave—I suppose it was a kind of involuntary retreat, a giving of ground, so as to gain a moment's more gaze. Then I should have to attend to the "Excuse me, Sir, closing time." I can't say why I wanted to have that last glance. Stained glass is not my specialty, of course, and my whole interest in St. Aidans, or, for that matter, in any Gothic building, had long lain on and in the ground plan. My start, disproportionate in any case, was double when the voice I was already expecting with an irrational tension, spoke at my shoulder not a command, but a question.

"It is a puzzle, isn't it?"

The voice, too, was not a verger's. I was startled, but my chief surprise was at myself—I felt strangely irritated. (I see now, that I should have understood what underlay this irritation, unprovoked, and, I think I may also say, uncharacteristic: irritation in the nonirritable is almost always a sympton of an unconscious malaise.) I tried to conceal my discomposure by the simple but crude device of refusing to lower my glasses. Then, as the best nonoffensive defense that I could muster, I replied, "The pattern *qua* pattern is clear enough."

I hoped the questioner might only be walking by, on his way out. If so, he could be merely a talkative casual who felt he must say something apposite to anyone he passed. My tone was deliberately flat, for I hoped he would take it to confirm my stance and construe both rightly: that I had no need for a gossip or a guide. "That's the puzzle" showed, however, that I had been mistaken; he had taken my attempt to disengage as a query-invitation. I still remained steadily gazing up at the patterned trefoiling. It should have discouraged him, but actually the effect proved contrary.

"One can have no doubt," went on the voice at my left shoulder, "that there is an unmistakable design up there. The actual way to follow it is the difficulty. Of that final trefoil, the topmost aperture contains, you see, some enwrought pattern in medallion pot metal."

I could not prevent my idle irrationally irritated curiosity from wondering whether my self-appointed companion also had a pair of strong binoculars? Otherwise, how could he detect the tiny ensconced fragment of involved glass fragments seventy feet from the floor on which we stood? Involuntarily, behind the mask of my field glasses, I swiveled my eye. He had none. But my surprise at his native vision, or acquired knowledge of the cathedral was swallowed up by a stronger surprise—surely, the man who was accosting me was the same man who had already surprised me by turning from an apparently casual sight-seer into the organist? At his first appearance he had seemed to shun me as much as I had given him a wide berth. Then he had seemed to be casually pacing the stones; next, he was master of that very odd, very moving organ, and now he was offering me his company and perhaps his problematical knowledge. Meanwhile he continued gazing at the summit of the clerestory window. My ill-controlled attention felt it had leave to wander—surely here was a puzzle odder than that high-water-mark flotsam of glazing.

I watched him now, deliberately though still obliquely. Yes, his interest seemed really to be in the glass—an interest evidently greater than mine. And certainly, now that I saw him close at hand, his face—turned up toward and lit by the late light from the high window—looked scholarly. Forehead, cheekbones, nose bridge, all high; eyes, cheek furrows, chin notch, all deep. Yes, I said to myself, the scholar's mask, right enough; though, perhaps, worn a trifle self-consciously—for example, that brush of white hair, its fringe making contact with the upsweep of hawk's-winged eyebrows. Eyebrows, I remember thinking to myself in my defensiveness, are to the scholarly make-up what mustachios used to be to the military's. However, by that time, I need hardly say, my interest in my would-be informant had swiveled me wholly around. He, however, though he continued talking, did not turn to me but continued looking aloft.

"The two other trefoils, the right and left, are more difficult to decipher, being in the nature of accompaniments. If the theme given in the center is mastered, then the others will fall into place, not otherwise."

I lowered my binoculars. As a mask, I owned with a smile at my exclusiveness, they would serve no more and, as an aid to decipherment, they had failed no less.

"Well, what is your interpretation?" I asked, with a distinct flavor of challenge rather than request in my tone. The fact that I had suspected him of being a common sight-seer and had found myself mistaken when he revealed himself as a remarkable if unique organist, had, I must own, not reassured me at all. Unfortunately, all scholars are now specialists, and the fact that a man shows himself an authority in one field causes him to be treated as a worse trespasser than a general ignoramus if he strays into another. His answer, I own further, confirmed my suspicion. He swung around. Any fine physical movement is for us men of the detached surface mind startling, unwelcome, ostentatious. I could not help feeling then that the gesture was a trifle theatrical. He pointed to the tower floor.

"As above, so below."

The archaic quotation suited too well the stately action.

"This is not a Hermetic Temple," I countered. I felt I

had a right to warn him I could recognize the pattern of pretension.

"Well, when reformers capture a stronghold of an ancient faith they seldom trouble to do more than change the flag."

This neat reversal of a famous Dean's famous epigram startled me, I own, into a less suspicious attention. He took his advantage at once but not at all figuratively, indeed actually in his stride. For with a swift movement he was now standing right under the bell hoist vault between the four tower arches. He wasn't looking tc me for a further reply; he was looking at his feet.

As I followed, he swung his hand around. "You see the maze here. The flagstones are set in an interwound pattern."

I was, of course, familiar with these and knew the accepted archaeological theories—the tracks of the fertility spring dances and the Sun-gates magic of the so-called "Trojan Game."

"That's common enough," I said. "Ely and several others are finer, and in East Anglia you can still find the earth-balk originals outside a number of villages." I dreaded that he was going to launch out into some "esoteric" fantasy.

He only answered, however, "They are frequent enough to be dismissed without an explanation. Why should a pagan fertility pattern be brought in, and be wrought into a church dedicated to sex repression and sex sublimation?"

I was not at all inclined to enter upon that kind of argument, and evidently he did not expect a reply.

"But the trefoils are the question, and have the first word of the answer." He did not, however, on saying this, return to our original viewpoint. I thought he was going to take up his old position, but, stepping back into the nave, he turned again to the right. I saw him dip through the little southwest postern. I followed—why I did, when I could have escaped, I am not sure. Probably what really moved me to go after him was that in the opposite direction I caught sight of the verger shuffling down the nave, obviously on his way to clear us out and lock the western doors. I certainly was not sure that this organist could give me any information I should have accepted as information, but perhaps I felt a vague intuition that if he were keen enough on his subject, and indifferent enough to his audience to follow the one and leave the other, the other might as well follow. By the time I had put myself through the double swing doors, he was going right once more, and so had reached the big western porch and the outer side of the main door.

"The sun is just right," he remarked, hardly turning, as though he was sure I would be at his heels. "You cannot actually see it at any other hour of the day."

"It," I presumed, from the line of his attention, was something on what looked like a bare slab of stone on the porch's north side, one of a series which made a plain surface between two belts of decoration. The stone, naturally, was considerably weathered, which may excuse me for missing any clue for a moment. Then, sure enough, under the sharp contrast of light and shade made by the level sun's ray cast obliquely on the stone, I could see that he was pointing out something—some sort of scrawl, perhaps a rude design, perhaps graffiti.

"All three," he remarked, "are ultimately needed, as three notes are required to make a chord. But, nevertheless, each will work of itself, though only together can they give the full clue."

I pulled myself together. "This, too, you can find at Ely, Peterborough. . . . Very interesting, I own, and I did not know of this one. But, of course, they are only line drawings, made by the medieval masons when working out an 'elevation' such as a West front."

" ' "Nothing but is never true," came the dominie's reply.' "Probably they did help the master builders to rear the West front, but what is the West front itself for? The pattern is the clue."

I can plead that any authority doesn't like being treated as a pupil—wrong, I own, but almost as invariable as a natural law. I can also plead, particularly, that I, being an authority who had advanced a number of advanced and hotly contested views on Gothic, was the type of man who, again wrongly and most commonly, is apt to be acutely suspicious of speculation which goes beyond even that shadow of proof which foreruns discovery.

"Prove it," was, then, a natural if somewhat curt challenge.

"Thank you." He did not seem daunted; on the contrary, pleased. "I can and will, if you'll comply," he added.

"How?" seemed sufficiently noncommital. But he took it to give him leave literally to take hold of me. He swung me, too surprised to hold my ground, until I was squarely before the face of the etched ashlar.

"Look at it closely," came the voice over my shoulder. "Start at the upper left hand corner."

It was an obvious place. If the drawing was a scratched

outline of what the West front might have been intended to be, then here was the northwest gable.

"Now, follow the design, right, carefully." And, to make me comply, I felt a thumb and finger press gently against the base of my skull, with just that point of pressure which the dentist's headrest applies.

The surprise at being so handled and the queer association with dental submission, I think, accounted for my yielding. I own I am not fond of being touched by strangers. There may, too, have been something in the contact that prevented what would otherwise have been my normal reaction. Whatever the reason, I did not shrug myself free and so found, under this delicate but compelling guidance, my head being gently swung up and down, while my neck was swiveled so that my eye might follow the etched design.

When I reached the end of the top of the design, my eye was led, in the same way, down its right side, across the base, up the left side, and then, once again, but on a lower tier of lines, across the front. My compulsory director had ceased to talk, of that I was aware faintly, but only faintly, because I was much more aware of something positive but, in spite of that, far harder to define, even to myself. The nearest I can get to it is to say that I was becoming giddy. And yet the word giddiness is very far from *le mot juste* for my state of mind. For, firstly, I felt uncommonly firm—the very opposite of vertigo. I felt the vibrant firmness of sure momentum which one feels in a yacht, when it goes cleanly over onto a full tack and has plenty of "way," or the firmness one experiences in large high-powered cars when the top gear slips in smoothly and one forges ahead on a wide-open road.

I think I can go a step further in trying to describe this strange, but strangely pleasant, state of consciousness which was spreading through me, spreading along my body and limbs from my head, as quiet ripples spread down from the mouth of a fiord and run up to the shore of every branching inlet. In ordinary states of consciousness we are always aware of making some sort of effort (how much, how often, I have realized since that experience!) to keep steady, to preserve a tiring rigidity. The bellows of the lungs are swelling and drawing at ribs and thorax; packed against them the heart is thrusting and pulling. The coil of the intestines turns, shifts, and sags like a large snake in a sack. The engine of the body, on its frail pelvic bedplate, throbs and drums against its casing. Poised on this casing, with an insecure foothold by the funnel, we try to keep a steady lookout.

Now I had begun to become aware, since I had been looking attentively at the design etched on the wall, and increasingly, as I had been tracing it out, following it serially with my eye, that the quiver of the body had not stopped, but somehow had ceased to require counterbalancing, counterchecking. I don't know how long this—if I may so call it —exercise lasted. I think I must have gone over and around that pattern several times—perhaps quite a number. One thing, however, I was able to reckon; each time a "round" was completed, the tension in myself (how high it had been I had never suspected) was lowered. Finally I could perceive I had reached a certain sea level or datum line, for I no longer felt the slightest wish in either direction—either to stop this curious behavior and get away or to continue it for its very strange but very distinct pleasurableness.

At that moment I heard the voice again at my ear and at the same time became aware that the touch on my neck had been lifted.

"That is part of the meaning—at least as much of it as can be made out, using only this part of the rendering."

The remark is, of course, far from self-evident; I can see that, as I put it down. Indeed, listening through the rational mind, I realized the outward senselessness of the words which I was hearing. But a deep pervading part of my mind, some profound understanding which was not confined to the reason, or even the brain, but which suffused and possessed the whole body, this larger consciousness had experienced under the speaker's guidance and so knew what he meant. The experience which I had had while swinging my head to follow those scratched lines on the stone, though not an experience I had ever had before (and so I had no words to describe it), was so complete, so massive, that I needed no more argument. Instead, I swung slowly around and, turning my back to the drawing, sat on a low stone ramp which, some two feet off the ground, terminated the great western alcove's bands of concentric arches.

My guide still stood his ground, so we were face to face, though I had to look up at him. And it was a look up in more than a physical sense. For I could see clearly now that what I had taken for theatricality or, at the best, a certain self-consciousness of drama, of presentation, now struck me as an actual authentic dignity.

"I know when we met you thought I was a busybody—an odd organist who wanted also to ape the antiquarian."

I saw further, whoever he might be, that he was not the man to be put off by courteous disavowals.

He hardly waited for the conclusion to form in my mind before adding, "I know, also, that under the antiquarian's dread of deceit, the fear of being taken in, is a real desire to decode the truth, to be taken in, in another sense, into the authentic arcana. Yet there are tides . . ."

Indeed, there are, and my sudden turn from suspicion to trust had passed its flood and was as rapidly ebbing. I felt that my strange sensation could only have been a slight vertigo, brought on by his really quite impertinent handling. I wished only to get away.

This feeling became acute when he went on, "Any other day of the year you might have missed everything."

"Because I should not have had the privilege of your guidance?" I questioned. The question was, of course, only a "discourtesy" question. I can say such a recoil was not normal to me, and—as a reaction or recoil—I believe it is partial evidence that, in the moments before, I had undergone some psychophysical experience from which temperament was attempting an "overbalanced" recovery. My opponent--I had almost said—well, my companion, refused to be challenged and thrown back to the part of a beaten-off boarding party.

He continued to remark quietly, more to himself than to me, "There is no chance; so to say 'coincidence' is to say nothing. I will therefore only note that it happens that only on this afternoon of the year—an afternoon naturally often overclouded, since it is the twenty-ninth of September—does the sun as it declines cast a ray at the precise angle which, striking obliquely on the stone you have been scanning, permits the pattern scored on it to be visible through the weathering of centuries. And this is the very day on which a visitor catches sight of the second clue in the topmost trefoil of the southwestern clerestory window. You will own that I owed you my services, considering the day." His voice was now specifically addressing me.

"What day?" The ignorance of my answer was due also, I suppose, to the slight giddiness I had suffered, as a slight shock will disturb one's memory momentarily.

His answer: "That's all the better. If you did not come here 'to keep the day,' then I may take it that others arranged it," left me even more bewildered. But when he added, "Now, to clinch it, let's step back into the cathedral," I was awake enough by then to point out, "The door was locked for the night almost as soon as we left."

He only answered, over his shoulder, "To one who knows a cathedral it is never locked—as, to the ignorant, it is never open. Like all true mysteries it is locked only to outsiders."

The last part of the sentence I would probably have resented because of its sententiousness, if something more remarkable had not caught my attention; the speaker had disappeared. I could, however, still hear distinctly enough the words which followed, "Come over to this south side of the porch."

I moved into the shadow of its deeply recessed clusters of shafting. Still I couldn't see him. "Now, stand on the ramp." I stepped up on the low stone benching. A hand touched me and drew me behind a pillar into a dark coving. I heard a latch click and hinges turning. "The passage is sufficiently narrow, you need not be afraid of stumbling, and won't want a light. So close the door as you pass through."

I passed in, and the small door, which I felt but could not see, at once hasped itself behind me. Ahead of me the voice went on talking gently and, in the stone cleft in which we were moving, every word, though not much above a whisper, came clearly back to me. The back of my hands brushed a smooth stone wall at each side. It was not groping, when touch was so unbroken and footing so level. And, even when the floor began to rise, each step seemed to meet one's foot as surely as a ladder's rungs. So we covered some three hundred steps perhaps. Once we turned at right angles. This unexpected and literal penetration into the structure of the great silent building had quite restored my mood of open, if somewhat amazed, interest. Whatever unsubstantiated theories might be held by the strange fellow ahead of me, there was no doubt he knew his way about the cathedral and was giving me an unexpected insight. I heard another latch click ahead, and light poured down past us. When, however, we stood out in it, it was really a twilight, an afterglow thrown from a huge window whose massive mullions sprang from a broad sill level with our heads. We had emerged, I could judge from the sense of space given by exhausted echoes and faint perspectives of light, onto the extreme western end of the south clerestory passage. I guessed his purpose but doubted its use. "That top trefoil can be seen better from the nave floor," I remarked.

And, indeed, that was understating the fact. The coving

of the stone tracery was itself so thick that, standing, as we were now, immediately under it, those uppermost fragments of mysterious glass were quite invisible to us. We could see only a faint mottling of color thrown on the upper lip of the stone mouth, deep in which the medallion jewelry was fixed, filtering obliquely the last western light. His reply, however, was to repeat the ancient maxim, "As above, so below." And as he said it a small ellipse of light appeared on the breastwork which screened the narrow wall on which we stood from the nave, forty feet below. I looked at the little elongated disk of light (it was thrown from a small flashlight which my guide was holding), and, sure enough, there was cut in the broad chamfer of the balustrade, which faced us like a stone reading desk, an engraved reproduction of the medallion maze-pattern up out of sight in the trefoil above us. The ellipse shifted.

"And here"—the light darted and paused, first on one side of the central engraving and then on the other—"Here are the even more obscure patterns which you saw in the right and left trefoils." He was certainly correct in that, for my memory is very retentive of pattern, and was helped in this question by the fact which I had noted when on the nave floor—these two "supporting" patterns were similar—the only difference between them being that the pattern of one was a pattern in which the line came in from the left, while in the other the line began its involutions from the right. They were "mirror images" of each other.

"They were kind, the original masons," went on the soft tone, in this fluted place more like an echo of very distant speaking than a face-to-face voice. "They do not wish to exclude anyone who will show real interest. In fact, they are always looking out for those they may welcome. Once you are really responsive to the signal flown aloft, then, when you have climbed as close as you can to its call, they leave the message where you, but no casual curioso, can find it."

"But," I questioned, "even now?" For though the graven lines were unmistakably sharp (here were no doubts introduced by the weather's random palimpsests), yet the whole enigma was not a whit more communicative when one stood gazing at it, less than eighteen inches from one's nose, than when one craned up at its rendering in glass almost eighty feet above one's head.

"*Solvitur ambulando*," the voice was nearly a whisper now or a sigh. "And that will prove the final solution, in the deepest sense. But the first step to that is *solvitur circulando*. Permit me again to direct your attention."

This time I voluntarily submitted. "Please place your right and left index fingers on the beginnings of the two engraved coils to your right and left." I obeyed. "Follow these by touch," he said. Meanwhile he kept the ellipse of light on the central pattern with one hand, and with his other gently manipulated my neck, so that, following these impulses, my head swung, repeating the lines of the maze. Almost at once I felt come over me again the strangely significant, soothing effect. But this time it was far stronger. Perhaps it was because I was now following a curved rather than a rectangular pattern; perhaps because while my head swung, my hands and arms were counterpointing the central theme. I can only say that whereas on the porch I had felt as though a new sense of mental balance was controlling and ordering my body, now the whole body, trunk and limbs as well as head, seemed to be taking part in the new expressive pattern. Then I was balanced and felt as though I could never slump, lounge, or shuffle again. But now I felt as though the body would never again have to be borne, however athletically. It would bear itself: it was an imponderable, a field of force, not a coil of machinery. As to my mind, I might almost say that after a few rhythms I felt as though it had passed into the maze. I was not an outsider tracing a pattern—rather, I was one of the rhythms of that pattern, given meaning and purpose by moving within its comprehensive order. I was living, moving, and having my being in the actual dynamic design which keeps all things, from atom to heart-beat, in an interwoven dance.

I did not move when the exercise was finished but stood, with my fingers touching the centers of each ancillary maze, my eyes fixed on the focus of the central one. A single wish was present in my curious and complete content—not by any shift of attention to lose this amazing direct sense of wholeness, of the lack of any conflict or striving, not to step back into the old throbbing, knocking, thwarted flutter and thump of life. Now that I knew, with a profound kinesthetic intuition, I must—it was my one ordinarily conscious thought, my one contact with my old acquisitive-defensive self—hang on to this knowledge. I simply must not lose this gnosis. So, though the voice was hardly more than the sound made by a shell close to the ear, I did start a little. The words also shook the mood I was clinging to. "That is enough."

My intellectual ego rushed back, breaking these new extensions of understanding which were lifting me to a selfless, wordless knowledge, rushed back, under the excuse of protecting me from exploitation, from ignorant patronage, from some charlatan's hypnotic trick. So pride can always blind true vision. But my guide evidently knew my limitations. Having lifted me out of the groove I had settled in, he did not provoke the aroused ego with more words. He conveyed our next step, not by tongue but by step. I heard the soft sound of his retreating feet and followed them. My critical spirit loosed its hold and, as far as I thought of anything or foresaw anything, I thought we would be returning to the west porch. But after the clerestory doorway closed behind us and we had made our descent of the internal stairway, when the lower little doorway clicked ahead it did not admit, I could see, the last glow of the day but a dusk hardly lighter than the gloom in which we had been stepping.

My guide must have taken another of the many divergent tunnel passages in the vast walls; for we had emerged, I could see, into a considerable space, dark on every hand except the right. There some sort of huge opening glowered. I should have known my bearings but I had, I suppose, lost that specific sense of direction in the sense of some much larger drift in things: as the carrier pigeon, it would seem, depends on its sensitiveness to the earth's magnetic field and so disregards and must disregard all ordinary sensory clues. My sensory clue came from another cast of the flashlight. I saw the oblique beam was thrown on the floor. The flash made it clear—we were back under the great western tower.

"This time," said the voice which, if possible, sounded softer and more diffused away from the walls—"this time, please follow me." The torch had been switched off and, even when my eyes had adapted to the deepened dusk, I could only see in most uncertain outline a column of darkness, which stood against gloom almost as dark. "Don't strain to see me; just look in the direction I move." He was right. Had I tried to gauge whither his dark figure was moving I should certainly have remained in doubt but, as it was, by an almost casual glance, I was aware that he was moving and, so easy and total was my attention as I watched, that I found I was keeping pace with him. Not until I had been so "in train" for some little while did my rational mind even begin to ask what we were doing or even how. Then I realized I was moving and turning in a certain defined area. I saw the glimmer of the great arch time and again frame the figure I was following.

Yes, we were threading the full-size maze delineated in the floor stones, that maze at which we had been looking, perhaps an hour ago, perhaps less, as the sun had been setting. The pacing came to me quite naturally, so that I hardly glanced for guidance but let some inner beat tell me when to turn and when to advance. For the third time I felt, but twice as strongly, the sense of being caught up into the real basic rhythm of things—swept from the beach on which the breakers swirl in confusion out into the deep, where the swell of the ultimate ocean moves in an inexhaustible process. I heard a voice say, "Once," and I noticed I could no longer hear the whisper of feet preceding my own; also, my eyes no longer found the faint impression of a leading figure ahead of me.

It made no difference. The rhythm, once learnt, took control itself. I ceased to look for outer confirmation of the inner prompting to pace and repace. In perfect kinesthetic knowledge, one made the curves, passes, involutions, reverses, as dancers may dance in the dark and in silence. Yet it was not merely the memory of a single lesson, rather it was one's whole ancestral frame recalling its primal rhythm and spring —swirl of the fish in water, volute of bird in air, plunge of the diver, leap of athlete. It would be impossible to say how long we paced, for, as one light wave can eclipse another and where they meet appears darkness, so, when a beat is found precisely equal to the beat of life and growth and movement, time, too, is canceled by its question being at last answered. Conscious time, I now realize, is caused only by a creature going out of step and so becoming sadly aware of Past, when things chimed, and of Future, when things will click but always being shackled in a Present where events only clash.

At last, the process was self-completed. For it only confirmed my own inner realization—the wonderful agreement now established between inner instant expectancy and the outer event—when the voice said at my side, "So, and so only, can we unloose the tension, resolve the complex, unravel the knot of the self. Now you are nearly free, and your frame is almost ready to be your expression and not your limitation. These buildings, like all supreme architecture, are a therapy in stone. Here is wrought the static pattern, here is laid down the plotted course, which, if followed by the living creature, will set it free. The Greek, being less entoiled, could deliver the body-mind by sight alone, and he who brooded on the faultless proportions of the Parthenon might in a static silence know liberation—though when he moved it vanished from him, as he passed out of the bright sharp shadow that it cast into the confused twilight of a world of growths. But our race, which wrought the lancet arch, worked with it because it required a stronger therapy and also demanded a more radical and abiding change of life. We must move, if we are to be delivered, and we must aid ourselves in our escape not only by sight but by sound, not only by the written score but the heard melody. Gothic truly may be mocked and marked down, if judged only by the eye. There, perhaps, the Hellene is the highest. But pure sight can never deliver those more conscious of their captivity. If you would worship, and be saved by your worship, you must do so where your soul can work out its salvation, can draw itself up out of the pit of self-consciousness into which it has fallen by that threefold cord of the senses. Kinesthetic and full of conflict, auditory and longing for resolution of discord: you need to do more than to know by seeing: you must see, hear, and feel, and, so knowing, be able to act on your knowing. Then your knowledge will be a springing gnosis in your very body and its bones."

Perhaps he spoke all that speculation in a single phrase; perhaps he said nothing—only thought what I was thinking; perhaps he did not think rationally but only held a frame of thought, a state of mind, while I filled in with an argument our actual experience. Perhaps it was necessary we should pause while I rationalized, soothed with a shift of logic the last questionings of my analytic mind. In any case, I know that after a few moments, which I have so to account for, my memory, and what we did, again becomes quite definite. He moved out into the nave, and I followed. But we did not walk down it. We started out, going northeast, so passing through the third arcade into the north aisle, then curving away from the north wall, repassing through the nave's north arcade, so, describing an arc, arriving at the entrance to the rood screen. Thence, turning westward, we repeated the pattern in reverse and on the south side, so finding ourselves once more back under the tower arch.

"So the great nimbus is described," the voice said as we paused. "Now not only are you opened by the releasing rhythms which have unshackled you but you have taken on and endued yourself with the rhythmic form of this great place, and it is open to you."

I understood enough to know that he was right. Again we set out on another stage of our vast journey, a journey so long that beside it all the traveling I have done in my entire lifetime has been merely shuffling from one room to another. We strode together silently; this time abreast and straight down the length of the nave, till again we were at the rood screen entrance. The gate was only latched, I think. It yielded to his touch and closed with a whisper behind us. The sweep of heavy curtain hanging behind also seemed only to indicate the silence lying ahead, as we passed into the sanctuary.

I have never heard such silence and I believe that it can never be brought about by relaxation or emptiness. The desert of sound, like the desert seen by the eye, is not a complete void or even an unrelieved level. Rather, they are randoms filled with irrelevant incident. The normal silence of the deserted place is, I might almost say, easygoing. It lies relaxed; and, in a great cathedral, when all contemporaries have gone (and I have been in many at such hours), there is an atmosphere of unvigilant carelessness. The great body, with its bones of masonry, its flesh of timber, its skin of lead and glass, lies relaxed and, as a man stretched in reverie will shift or sigh, off and on, so the giant frame will shift and creak. The silence in that sanctuary on that eve of September the thirtieth was not the absence of sound. True, no sound reached us. The small town pressed upon the narrow close. Granted that night had fallen, yet people would still be up and about, discharging that constant vibration of small penetrating noises which accompany human movement.

When I listened for them, I was aware of the positiveness of the silence. It was around us like a wall. It was as emphatic as though someone had plugged the ear with a finger or, rather—and this, I believe, may come near to the actual truth of this intense experience—as though the place had become a breathable vacuum in which a man might live, but into which and across which no sound wave could move. Once again there occurs to me the analogy of the two light waves meeting and resulting in apparent darkness. The place was holding its breath in some tremendous expectancy and, by an intensity of attention toward some approaching event, was holding off every possible present interruption. Some supersonic intensity was here, in the presence of which no auditory sound could be sustained. We ourselves seemed to make no suspicion of stir as we moved forward.

I could see the tall shade of my companion move to the right. I followed closely. We had passed into the stalls. The choir is not large. Now that the console of the new organ has been brought down into the stalls, the organist's bench almost abuts at right angles on to the dean's. I felt a hand raise me into this east-facing stall. I was aware that my companion was moving on to take his place at the keyboard. Then the immense atmospheric pressure of positive silence seemed, not to lift (for no other sound of any sort was audible), but, rather, to fissure, and through this momentary cleavage, as in a midnight thunderstorm the line of the lightning will slit the blackness, I could hear the words, "Remember, all is movement, all is sound. If the Living Word becomes too insistent, join your hands, and you will be able to sustain it."

I had not the faintest intellectual notion of what was about to take place. But I realized, subconsciously—perhaps more with my body than with any part of my mind—that now I had been, as it were, not only "wound up" within my own frame; that all its wandering, streeling impulses and swayings, all my divagations, chatterings and skiddings, had been brought into perfect spin like a sleeping top, but, also, that in the process of so preparing me I had been moved toward the heart of the energy—whatever it might be—into which I should, when my revolutions were sufficiently high, find myself ready to be engeared. I repeat, I do not know whether this was in any way a mental, or a conscious, or a paraconscious notion. My whole memory of this is, I believe, far closer to animal memory than to human, and by that I mean that as, for example, an elephant is not always thinking over the wrong a cruel keeper did it, forty years ago, biding the time when it may attack him, but, on the contrary, suddenly seeing him again the two times link up, the years of forgetting are forgotten, the wrong is as fresh as on the day of its infliction, and the keeper is trampled, though meanwhile he may have become kind and have no fear, so I, if I am to remember what took place, I can do so as clearly, but only if I also dive into the physical mood I then felt going below the surface sequence of my normal memory.

So I stood as though waiting for a service to begin. I can, however, remember that I did feel a slight halt of surprise when, after a few moments during which I drew myself to attention, my guide, whom I could sense rather than see in front of me, did not, as I had come to expect, sound a note. I strained my ears, but they only sang their own inner high-pitched hiss under my effort. And this was stopped suddenly, not by sound or by sight, but by feeling. A violent pain shot through my palms. I snatched up my hands from the broad smooth desk on which they had been resting. They were stung as though by a hornet. I could have wrung them with the keenness of the pang. I can best describe the pain by saying it was the kind of sting a bat which has failed to give "drive" to the ball that has been struck gives to the hands which are wielding it, and makes the wielder drop it as though it were a live terminal. In my pain I clasped my hands involuntarily, as one holds an injured limb. Immediately the atrocious stinging left them. Then I recalled my guide's counsel.

I stood like this, in the silence, a little while—enjoying, I suppose, the warm relief that follows a spasm of agony. Then my attention began to leave my hands for my feet. My soles were experiencing a gradually increasing crepitation—a "pins-and-needles" effect. It was not until then that I realized that the whole framework of the massive stalls must be vibrating intensely. Before I was able to think about this, and to wonder whether I was in any danger, I heard a whisper, "Now it is safe. The note has climbed past the danger point." Again I put my hands on the desk before me. Only a pleasant, curiously invigorating warmth flowed up through my arms and down through my feet. I realized that a tide of ordered sound must be pouring out from the organ, a supersonic melody that, passing the ear, spoke directly to one's whole physical frame. I was awere of a steady surge of harmonic vitality running through the whole structure of the building—as an electric current, finding no resistance in a coil, rushes smoothly in a completed circuit. Gradually the surge seemed to become a pressure. I felt it go deeper into me, as it were, as though, before, it had been only a surface tide or, at most, a foreign fluid which made its way through my body alongside my own human currents. It became a beat—faster than the wave beat of sound and pulsing behind the ear drums. It was a ripple that flowed faster than the arterial flood. A warmth that seemed to dilate them glowed in my hands and feet. I felt framed and held in my own massivity. I could not be sure I was holding the desk and standing on the floor. Something solid but fluid, flowing but firm and encompassing—as strong and undeflectable as a jet of water thrust with ten thousand tons' pressure—seemed not merely holding me but, equally, containing and contained by me.

I gave myself up to the sensation—the feeling of being no more than an eddy in a vast stream which formed, sustained, and would elucidate me.

Self-consciousness, however, reasserted itself. I found myself becoming perceptive, visually perceptive—I was experiencing that separation of the sense of sight, the human dominant sense which gives rise to "my point of view," from the undifferentiated sensum into which I had been swept. I saw the whole choir—not outlined in light—rather the shafting, arcading, capitals, spandrels, the springers, ribs, vaulting, bosses, were all transparent and, like an immense phosphorescent billow, glowing with an inherent flush that shone throughout the translucent mass. But this effect, though strangely wonderful, could not hold my attention against the invasion of another discovery, smaller but more personally startling. I was looking at the choir, there could be no doubt, but whence? Equally, there was no doubt—from some level little short of the capitals themselves—in fact, some twenty feet from the choir floor, above the canopies of the stalls.

My misgiving did not, however, become fear, for no sooner did apprehension begin to be felt by me than (as though a lowering of some psychic temperature checked the exultant current flowing through me and bearing me up) I began to settle, subside still further down until I could feel the hard floor under my soles again, and the burden of my weight upon my feet. That this was the explanation of the flow and ebb I felt, that it was an objective experience, I could gauge further. For no sooner did I feel this physical reassurance (and so my momentary fear left me) as I felt it go, once again I was raised in this current of energy. Now, too, I began to be aware of another sense responding. As I was already seeing—or, rather, some apprehension, which is above and beyond sight, was responding to the energy which was now informing every stone and timber around me—so, in the same enhanced or extended way, I now began to hear.

I was listening to a note which was running through the whole vast building's structure, and to which the great hollow place was responding like a struck bell. I was not reaching out to sense it, as though it were a note at the very limit of my apprehension. On the contrary, it was closer to me than the marrow of my bones: my bones were flutes through which the note was being blown. It was a diapason so pervasive and profound that one realized it must underlie all silence, were one but put in key to apprehend it. Terrible and fascinating, one felt that all one's wish was only to continue listening to it, though it was like a stanchless tide sweeping away, moment by moment, the poor sand and silt of one's personality. It resembled, in some way, a long exultant cry—an unending exclamation.

I know how banal *that* sounds; but let one who has heard that inexhaustible exultation say which was the stronger passion of the two it roused—fear or desire. No other feeling, no surprise, no critical detachment was left. Does a man overwhelmed by a simoom remark that the shriek of the rent atmosphere is a trifle off-pitch? If there had been about it the least hint of possible exhaustion, fluctuation, weakness, resignation, or even content, it would have seemed, perhaps, a sigh or moan as of the whole universe in travail. If it had had the slightest overtone of unsatisfied longing, it would have become the voice of an annihilating agony. But it had in it no trace of human weakness—either of the weakness of hunger or of that of satiety—the longing for a goal or the satisfaction in finding it. It forged forward, insatiable and inexhaustible, in the tide of its outpouring. It was, though certainly not a blind thing, the great dark wind that blows ceaselessly through the kindling stars, which are the blown embers which the primal Breath moves and makes glow.

It was conscious, it was consciousness, it was the authentic vibration of imageless thought—an awareness, as intense as it is impartial, of the being of every atom of the manifold. "O," I thought it cried. "O," the basic registration of experience. But "O," uncompleted, must end in poignancy. Balancing that longing, came, undergirding that vault of sound, the hum as of the dynamo of creation. "M." The sound was passing, utterly unimpeded, through everything: everything welcomed it, as plants welcome water, as lungs welcome air. Everything was sustained, rather, shaped by it, as—the million grains of the sand-spout rear their blinding column because the invisible air current drives them.

The circuits of harmonies swept from crypt to roofrib, tempering the flaccidlike steel, making every solid clear as crystal. The circuits swept laterally also. They sped with unobstructed effortless energy around the walls from the western doors to the high altar. My eyes rested there. The tide which I had thought could brim no higher seemed still to mount. Sound and sight at this range could keep separate no longer. They were fusing. My whole and total attention was drawn to where a heart of focal intensity began to form.

I saw the massive stone altar first begin to glow like a ruby; then it was a heart of liquid gold like a solid single-crystal chrysoprase: the gold intensified into ice-cold emerald and passed into the dark sapphire of an arctic sky; this again withdrew into a violet so deep that the visual purple of the eye itself seemed absorbed in that depth, that abyss of color in which sight was being drowned. And as this intensification of vibrancy seemed to sweep across the visible spectrum up to those ranges where energy absorbs all mass and that which can pierce the most solid is itself fine beyond all substance, so it seemed with hearing. That abyss of sound which I had been thinking of as only depth, it, too, seemed to rise or, rather, I suppose I was carried up on some rising wave which explored the deep of the height.

As the light drew toward the invisible, I experienced a sound so acute that I can only remember feeling to myself that this was the note emitted when the visible universe returns to the unmanifest—this was the *consummatum est* of creation. I knew that an aperture was opening in the solid manifold. The things of sense were passing with the music of their own transmutation, out of sight. Veil after veil was evaporating under the blaze of the final Radiance. Suddenly I knew terror as never before. The only words which will go near to recreating in me some hint of that actual mode are those which feebly point toward the periphery of panic by saying that all things men dread are made actually friendly by this ultimate awfulness. Every human horror, every evil that the physical body may suffer, seemed, beside this that loomed before me, friendly, homely, safe. The rage of a leaping tiger would have been a warm embrace. The hell of a forest wrapped in a hurricane of fire, the subzero desolation of the antarctic blizzard, would have been only the familiar motions of a simple well-known world. Yes, even the worst, most cunning and cruel evil would only be the normal reassuring behavior of a well-understood, much-sympathized-with child. Against This, the ultimate Absolute, how friendly became anything less, anything relative.

Yet those words hardly bring back more than a faint last shudder of animal fear. What I confronted, I can at least verbally recall, was something that went beyond all animal shrinking. Everything human in me recoiled from That, as the blind racial life within us flies to the grasp of physical agony rather than be lost in that void of annihilation. Yet the real anguish was caused, I could apprehend, not by a simple unanimous wish to escape. It was due to the conflict, the peril, being within myself. One part of me longed for the last film to disappear—for eye and ear, or rather that which listened and saw, that which was apprehending already beyond any capacity of response, to comprehend, to grasp and be grasped by that which now beat, an unfathomable ocean, against this last frail sandspit of separateness. One part of me, still rooted in my individual, human, animal life, feared, with that fear which will make the resolute suicide yet struggle as the water bursts into his lungs, that in an instant more my selfhood would be lost forever.

I felt the awful spasm of a creature suddenly made to sustain the pressure of two universes, its frail twofold nature the sole link between two primal energies—that of a life force forever seeking fresh forms and new experiences, forever desiring to forget and to discover, and an utter Being, possessed of all, for being the All, instant and absolute. Temporal and Eternal, for a moment I knew both, and for an instant sustained the anguish of belonging to neither. The small weary words, Heaven and Hell, chart on a miniature globe the two poles between which my being was held, but no words or trace of remembered feeling can now recall the utter force which these two opposites exerted on the atom caught between them. In finality, I can say that only then did I understand the fundamental—maybe—the eternal strength of consciousness even when reduced to the grotesque limitations of personality: only then did I grasp why the Universe, why the Eternal Reality, requires the individual, and will not be satisfied until all that can call itself "I" will dare to rise and recognize Him who is the Whole.

The carrying note dropped—the terrible vortex contracted and closed—the visible world reformed like thick ice over a well, sealing the shaft, making it safe for men to stand secure, unaware, over the abyss. The whole great building groaned as it settled again into its accustomed dead-weightedness. My hands and feet again stung, perhaps as agonizingly, but I was too stunned to wince and dumbly took the pain. My eyes were flooded with bruised and wounded visual purple.

"Come," said a voice beside me. A hand guided me along. We paused under a window through which a late-rising moon was throwing its light. My recovering vision rested on the lit opening. Gradually I made out the illuminated design. It showed a small dark human figure grappling with an overarching form of brightness, while underneath ran the words, "Like a Prince thou hast wrestled and hast prevailed."

We were outside in the dim close. "You need now never forget. If you will, you may try and convey what you now know. It is lawful, but no one can say if it is possible. Nor will you be unwise. When you would see whether you may recapture and transmit in words what you have experienced, when you reach the limit to which your description and memory will go, then, if you still feel the obligation to pass on what has been given you, sound then the note you have heard. It will be echoing in the back of your mind henceforward and will come when you call. Then once again you will know directly, and not by an ever-fainter recollection. But whether at that moment you will bring down the Eternal into Time or be drawn from Time into the Eternal, it is not for us small shuttles in the weaving to say or know."

When I reached the inn by the close gate he was gone.

Since my return I have been deciding what to do. My mind, of course, has fluctuated. There have been three principal choices. I could go back to St. Aidans and check up on my impressions—surely, I should? Such a story, even if it were all objective, should be carefully confirmed, and there was at least the chance of obtaining a witness. But somehow I knew that would serve little use. I could let the whole matter drop, treat the episode with any excuse I liked—an hallucination, a fantasy—something, anyhow, that I had a duty to disregard. Naturally, that was my strongest inclination. Indeed, I began to act on it. I actually returned to my routine, resumed my technical studies, went on with my opus, and let it be known that progress was being maintained. But it has proved vain. If a very unorthodox antiquarian may compare himself with the most orthodox of theologians, I felt myself like Aquinas after that mysterious Mass on St. Nicholas Day in the Chapel of St. Nicholas at Naples.

As I looked at my careful folios, with their data, arguments, deductions, their measurements, plans, scale charts, as I checked over my conclusions and thought of the theories I had labored half a lifetime to substantiate, and of the colleagues I had controverted, challenged, incited, informed—

what did it matter if I proved my point, my pinpoint of a proposition, that Gothic was more a rite than an architecture? I repeated to myself time and again, after some kind friend had called, asking me with encouraging interest if all was going well, the famous Thomine words, "Reginald, I cannot, for such things have been shown me that all that I have written seems but chaff," chopped hay which will nourish no one, and which a draft will scatter.

So I have come to the third choice and my final conclusion. I am availing myself of the leave given me to try and convey what I experienced. I realized, when I began this memorandum narrative, that I could hope for no reception from any scholar. Even had my antiquarian orthodoxy been unblemished, this statement must have blasted it forever. Yet knowledge is not for those who accept in its name the right to be pensioned off from life and actual contemporary experience. Outside the ranks of scholarship there may be those who, because they are human, have to face sometime what I saw and, because they have minds vital enough to sustain them exposed to the experiences of a changing world, they may be prepared to entertain new knowledge. If so, for them I make this effort, this exposure. But now, when I have written this account, I see it conveys nothing; it, too, is "but chaff."

So, because I have decided to make this attempt, because I have not succeeded, because I was told, when permission to attempt it was given, that there is one more possible resource which can be employed and that I have not yet used, now I am about to summon that aid. It is, as I was told, sounding in the depths of my mind like a phrase ready to be remembered. I will then once again draw myself up to my desk and get ready to transmit. If it comes through, then I am sure the written words will convey, if not that, at least the way whereby those who would read openheartedly may come to the Presence. If the wire will not carry the current, then, willingly, the vehicle will be flashed back to the source of power.

I draw in my breath. I feel the answer rising—I remember.

THE CAT, "I AM"

"Do YOU KNOW anything about Possession?"

"Well, it's nine points of the law."

"I don't mean possessing; I mean being possessed."

"By what? You don't mean. . . ?"

"I don't know. I wish to hell I did!"

The setting was conventional; a warm wood-fire in a soundly built, open fireplace. The room finely wood-panelled, modern without flagrant departure from tradition, panels alternated with built-in bookcases filled to the floor with books, their ordered book backs making the best of wall-papers. The two men matched. They might have been supplied by the furnishers with the room; each picked to fit the big easy chair in which he lounged in tweeds cut for lounging. They even had pipes in hand and whisky on the small table that was fitted into the central wedge, which was all the two overgrown chairs permitted in the fireplace area.

Comfort, good sense, physical fitness, wide, easy interests—there wasn't an object in the large, full-furnished, well-lit, freshly warm room that did not chorus that sequence of assurances. There was nothing that looked by any possibility askance—still less uncanny. There was nothing, either, that didn't sound the same: the crackle of the fire to give the traditional sense of well-being, the murmur of a dance tune from the radio to bring the modern assurance of a world well within call—a world telling you that it was having a good time and that ease, rhythm, fun, sensible sensuality—the five senses harmonized and put to a lilt—is all there is to know and all we need to know. There was no other sound to suggest any other possibility—except that one odd, incongruous but, thank heaven, still ambiguous word, Possession.

"It all may be accident, coincidence, contingency, or whatever it is that scientists use to erase writing when it appears of itself on our walls. I hope you'll tell me it is. I know one can see cyphers everywhere, as the wilder Baconians find them in any passage of Shakespeare. And, of course, many children," he bent forward and poked the fire with rather unnecessary force, "can see faces in the fire. Eidetic imagery, don't they call it? I hope you'll tell me it's just that or something of that sort."

"How can I tell you what it really is until you tell me what you think you have experienced?" Dr. Hamilton thought it no harm to show a little irritation. Innes had asked him over this evening but had never warned him he was wanted for a sideline opinion. That *is* irritating to any man who has done a long day's over-the-countryside work and not reassuring to a doctor who has watched for a number of years the way a nervous breakdown may open its attack and who knows perhaps a little more of the patient than he likes. It was bad and vexing that Innes hadn't said he felt a bit queer and would like to consult his friend and doctor. No harm friend and doctor being the same, provided patient and friend did not confuse *his* two parts.

Innes had always been a fairly normal if not a very attractive type—a sound if not very remunerative patient and a friend with whom one would play golf and dine more than one would share confidences. He looked sane enough, but of course those stable quiet fellows, if they ever fell off the high poop of their sanity, were apt to go right down and not come up again. But he must listen, not run on.

Innes was apologizing. "I'm sorry to have brought you around under false pretenses—at least I hope they are false. You see, I was sure they were. Every detail in itself is nothing—but together—"

Whatever it is, reflected Hamilton, that's sufficient evidence of strain. Innes is businesslike, and that's not a businesslike opening. Aloud he said, "All right. An outsider"—he deliberately did not say doctor—"is certainly a better judge than oneself as to whether any odd series of events has a real, objective connection. Fire away; spin your yarn, and I'll pull you up when I think you're making hookups where there aren't any." He felt he had used the right tone—not merely for Innes but for himself. For he always liked to be objective even with himself, and somehow that sudden opening of Innes', after what he'd thought was a cheerful pipe-drawing silence, had, he owned, shocked him—just the utter incongruity of the remark in this snug place from that commonplace man.

He was sure he had used the right tone as far as Innes was concerned. The man seemed relieved at once. Hamilton naturally shared his relief. His mind had already run ahead to the story's end. He knew now it was a little insomnia, domestic strain—a doctor has to diagnose the whole family of a patient—perhaps a few Freudian fear-dreams, perhaps a freak or two of amnesia. Yes, five to ten grains daily of dear old Pot. Amon. I'm young enough, he thought, to be returning to the old sound sedatives—not, of course, Pot. Brom—that was too lowering. Perhaps a little iron—often a touch of anemia gave one queer exhaustions and fancies.

But Innes was well under way. "They're the more intelligent and beautiful." Damn, he'd missed the beginning and mustn't show it. "He taps against that French window over there. And I go over and let him in. I've often sketched him as he grooms himself." Of course, it's a cat he has! "We've had him some six months. He isn't a success with the ladies. Of course, she should have known, if she had thought a moment. They can't be turned into lap-dogs or mannikins. He's himself—at least, I was sure—well, to go on. I call him 'I am'; he's so clear and emphatic. They're lovely, those Siamese with their pale blue, almost transparent eyes," he paused a moment, "and their smoky fur. But they have strong characters. Very temperamental, in fact. He got in some fine scratches on my wife." Innes laughed. "Tore her lace coverlets and silk pillows; actually bit the cook and of course tried to eat a squawking blackbird they're trying to tame and teach words to. Silly; let an animal be an animal, I say. Cook said the cat deliberately bit her but she's so deaf I expect she never saw that I Am was about—though Siamese have a step as audible as a dog's. I've often heard my wife saying to Cook, in a voice that certainly carries into the diningroom, 'Are you deaf?' She says Cook never even turns around and then says she's not deaf and Mrs. Innes shouldn't speak so indistinctly."

Hamilton was not interested in hearing a patient diagnose another patient's very different symptoms. But a description of domestic tensions could throw a valuable sidelight on the situation. He attended carefully as Innes went on. "It seems that just at the point where it would have been necessary to sacrifice the cat to save a major loss in the kitchen, I Am took himself off. I thought he'd gone for good, bagged by a passing hobo who saw there'd be a couple of meals to be got for his pelt. But in three or four days there was a tap on the bottom pane of that French window back there—I've never known another cat to do it—a smart little tap—no mewing—you could hear his claws click on the glass. That became a regular arrangement. I read in here after dinner, as a rule. Regular as clockwork, the tap would come at nine-thirty."

Hamilton glanced casually at his watch; it was nine. "I get up and let him in. He runs in and trots in front of me to the fire here. He waits till I'm settled again and then, after a look at the fire, to judge, I suppose, whether he's at the right distance from it, he settles down to groom himself. It's a regular ritual and takes considerable time: first the chest; then round the ears with the paws; next, paw-drill working between the pads; that's followed with big, side sweeps that get most of the coat clean; and the whole concludes with the most gymnastic pose. It must be good for the figure as well as for the fur. You hoist one back leg like a signal while, with the help of a front paw driven out behind you, you thrust your head forward and clean the fur right down on your tummy."

"Yes," said Hamilton, "yes," impatiently wondering why all this rather old-maidish cat-cataloguing. Then, with self-reproof, he realized that Innes must be spinning out his story, trying to gain time. He was edging toward some part of it that must be creepy. He was trying, with an accumulation of sane, simple, boring detail to give a setting of reassuring dullness to what had to come out at last. "Yes," Hamilton said encouragingly.

"Well," said Innes, "well, just four nights ago the tap came as usual. I got up, went over there, and I could see his misty-looking face waiting to be let in. As I opened the window, he hopped over the threshold and trotted ahead of me to the fireplace. I sat down. He chose his position, just about where your feet now are, gave a lick, and then, with that queer deliberate way cats have, as though he had suddenly remembered something he had been told but till that minute had all but forgotten, he got up again—he had never done so before—and went over there." Innes pointed to a bookcase which was almost opposite the French window and the lowest shelf of which was within an inch of the floor.

"There, almost touching the books, he began his grooming. I watched him a little and then went back to my book. I was reading in this chair. I suppose my attention was again disturbed by a slight tapping. The light, you see, is a good one." He pointed up to a powerful reading lamp which was standing behind them.

"Yes, good for the eyes," said Hamilton.

"It has, you see, a reflector, and this was throwing the light over my shoulder. I could see that the cat had come to the concluding phase of his drill. The hind leg was hoisted —the whole body and head assembled, as it were, around this raised ensign. I could see precisely what I Am was doing as his head was pointing this way. He was grooming the inside of his raised thigh, and I could also see what caused the small regular noise. Every time he swept the fur with his tongue, the upraised leg wagged and the hoisted paw, rising above his head, tapped on the book backs behind him."

Well, Hamilton could not help reflecting, all this parlor natural history might be reassuring, but it certainly doesn't seem to be leading anywhere.

"Well," continued Innes, suddenly becoming hesitant, "you see, from this position I could see exactly."

"Yes."

"I've long sight, you know?"

"Yes, yes."

"So there couldn't be any doubt. The books in that row are just as they were then." Innes suddenly got up, went to the bookcase, bent down, taking a volume from the ground shelf, turned round and handed it to Hamilton. Hamilton read aloud, *Called, I Come.*

"It may be coincidence." Innes again hesitated, as though turning over something in his mind and speaking mainly to himself.

"I don't think it is coincidence," answered the doctor. Then, with deliberate reassurance, "Really, you may take my word for it, there is nothing in *that.*" He'd often known quiet emphasis to work with excited patients.

"Good, good," Innes replied almost absentmindedly. "Then listen to this." He replaced the book and sat down again, still looking at the bookcase and no longer at Hamilton. "Of course cats are creatures of habit. What makes them change a routine, Heaven knows. Some little external accident, perhaps, psychologists would say. But once it is changed, the pattern goes on in the new place. The next night the tap came on time; the same entry was made. I was accompanied to the hearth here: then I was left, and almost but not quite, the same position as that of the night before was chosen for the grooming ritual. The cat placed himself with his back to the books and got to work, but it was against the row nearest to us, and not that farther one in which the volume named *Called, I Come* is standing. I read my book until once more the regular tapping disturbed me. I knew, of course, at once what it was. It was a distracting little sound: not sufficient to be annoying, but enough to take one's attention from the book and make one raise one's eyes, so that, over the top of the page, one could watch the toilet. The paw, hoisted over the top of the rhythmically moving head, was, under the strokes, waving to and fro; and, as on the night before, it was beating on the books immediately behind. Again I idly read the title indicated in this chance way, with this queer pointer."

Innes again got up, knelt down at the bookcase, but this time, didn't take out a book; instead he pointed with his finger and read out the title: *I Cross the Frontier.*

"It's a dull book," he said. "The other book is, of course, that sentimental anthology which had such a success a couple of years ago. This is simply a poor autobiography of one of my wife's old pioneer ancestors of whom she's pointlessly proud." He stopped again.

Hamilton felt he should put another layer of reassurance on the rather quaggy ground. "No," he said judiciously, "there's certainly nothing out of the common in that either

—there's not a shred of objective association between these two incidents, I'll warrant."

"You're sure?" asked Innes with an unhappy concern.

"Quite sure." The answer was professional. Hamilton now felt no doubt that this was no time for easy friendly speculation. He must be professionally authoritative. To himself he remarked: 'Certainly bromide: perhaps, too, castor oil—sometimes intestinal clog can . . .'

But the patient was proceeding. "I see your point: just those two points, mere incidents—yes, I know. Indeed, I'm sure they didn't disturb me. True, I remembered them, because—well, because I'm interested in cat psychology." He gave a feeble laugh. "All detail is important to a diagnostician, isn't it?" Hamilton gave only a Lord Burleigh nod. "I'm sure I'd have forgotten them, if . . . Well, the next night the same routine was followed. The usual tap, the entry, the walk to the fireplace, and the second thought that the better position was by the bookcase. But at that point a variation was introduced. It confirmed the psychologists: an outer stimulus altered the pattern. I think, indeed I'm pretty sure, I Am was just getting ready for his clean-up when his attention was distracted from himself. I can't be quite sure, for I only looked up when I heard a scrambling. He'd caught sight of one of those oddly inefficient but surprisingly nimble insects we used to call daddy longlegs. It was half-flying and half-hopping about. For some reason cats are easily aroused by them and, to chase them, even grooming or eating or sleeping by the fire will be instantly abandoned. Already the Siamese was boxing at it as it rose in the air and pouncing as it alighted on the carpet. But always the insect just managed to make a getaway. I watched the duel for a few moments, and then the daddy longlegs bobbed past a sweep of the cat's paw and skidded against the books. For a second it hung on to the top of a volume—the cat whirled round and sprang, and the fly, either driven by the impact of the blow or leaping away from it, shot into the space, of an inch or so, between the books and the shelf above them.

"That cat thrust its paw in, as far as it could reach. I watched, idly amused. It was so like an impatient human, groping for something he has dropped behind a chair or desk. You could almost hear I Am swearing under his breath. I let him struggle, sure that he'd give up in a moment and we'd both of us go back to our quiet concerns: he with his coat, I with my thoughts. But he didn't. I could just hear the fly faintly whirring behind the books, and maybe I Am could feel it buzz against his outstretched groping toes. Anyhow he redoubled his efforts. He pushed both front paws into the crack above the books. He wedged himself in and then, with his efforts, actually began to work a couple of volumes loose.

"I let him go on: such industry seemed to deserve not to be discouraged. Perhaps he had a purpose . . ." Again Innes paused. "Well, anyhow, this partial success encouraged him. He worked away and, sure enough, the two books fell out. Now he had breached the daddy longlegs defences. He thrust himself in, head and all, reaching behind the books, still straining to find his victim's retreat. It was a long reach, though—the books he had displaced were in the center of that bottom left-hand row, and, naturally, the fly retreated into the back corner of the shelf. The cat had, therefore, to push himself in and, in doing so, his hind leg, thrust out to give him drive, stamped right onto a page of a book he had thrown out and which was sprawling open.

"That was too much. My love of books won against my interest in natural history. I sprang forward, pulled him out by the scruff of his neck, and rearranged the shelf. But, in replacing the books, I noticed a vexing thing. I said I thought the cat had been distracted before he could settle down to his evening wash. Well, that was painfully obvious. His hind foot, the one with which he had done the big push, had obviously been still muddily damp. For it had left a complete imprint on the margin of the page. I brought the book to the light, hoping I might be able to wipe it clean before the mud dried in."

Innes stopped. Putting his hand down beside him in the chair, he fished up a volume, opened it, and put it on the broad arm of the chair near Hamilton's. Hamilton leaned across. True enough, on the outer border of the left-hand page, about halfway down, was a blur of mud stain rather like a large, clumsy asterisk stamped with a blunt rubber pad. "And you see," went on Innes, "the page is further spoiled." That was clear, too. One of the cat's hind claws had found purchase in the paper and had made a little tear right through the page. The two men looked for a moment at the damaged leaf. Then Innes remarked in an altered tone, "Do you notice anything else about this page?"

Hamilton scanned it. "No?" he questioned. Innes sighed, but all he actually said, as he remained looking down at the open book, was: "This game fish is not only deaf but so stupid that, though it can move quickly out of range when alarmed and then keep concealed, it seems unaware of his presence: when, after four or five days of such approach, during which he has become more and more clearly visible, he can stand right over the pool and spear it easily."

"You see," he said, looking up from the page, for he had been reading from it, "what I may perhaps call the cat's asterisk or sign manual is put alongside that passage . . ." He looked up at Hamilton, but the doctor had put out his hand and taken the book. "Big Game Fish," he read out to himself. "Well, that's healthy, outdoor sport."

Paying no attention to the comment, Innes completed his own sentence . . . "and the cat's claw, like an accent stroke, is notched against the line which runs, 'After four or five days of such approach . . .' "

Hamilton cleared his throat. "Really, Innes," he said, closing the book and putting it aside, "you must take my opinion. There is nothing in all this. Nothing at all." Innes turned his head away. "Now, don't think I'm going to be stupidly back-slapping and tell you just not to have damn-fool fancies. But, first, you must take my word for it, my professional word, that all these little incidents which have," he paused for a word, "have so annoyed you, are, in *themselves,*" he stressed the last word, "nothing, absolutely nothing."

Innes had sunk in his chair. Hamilton hurried a little; he must rouse the man. "And, secondly, I assure you, I give you my word, that you were right, very right to talk it all over with me. I want particularly to assure you that I've come across plenty of cases like this, plenty; quite common in my practice, quite common. Nothing to be alarmed over, if they're understood. Due to strain, you know, subconscious of course. Quite easy to deal with, quite, taken in time, as you've taken it."

All that Innes said in reply was, as he turned round slowly and fixed his eyes on the doctor, "Then I may tell you all?"

"Why, of course, naturally, naturally, that's half the cure, you know, especially when we've already decided that we know the source of the little trouble—just strain, strain that's making these queer little subjective associations appear as associations, which an onlooker can see are here," he pointed quite gaily to his own head, "and not there." He made a flourish which included the book, fireplace, and bookcase.

Indeed, he might have run on with his reassuring patter had not Innes interrupted him with, "Well, the next thing was worse. Perhaps I'd have lacked nerve to tell you if you hadn't told me to go ahead—at least after the way you've treated evidence which seems to me fairly objective. For this, I know, isn't."

That's bad, thought the doctor; it's a developing hallucination.

"The next night—the fourth," Innes remarked parenthetically, "there was the usual tap at nine-thirty. How he knows the time, I don't know; but then, I know now that I know nothing."

"Go on," said Hamilton in a quietly commanding voice.

"Well, he does know that, I know for certain," said Innes almost defiantly. "I confess I went to the window for the first time with something like real uneasiness. Damn it, I'm sure you'd have felt the same if you'd been seeing things as I couldn't help seeing them."

For a moment Hamilton felt, emotionally—not rationally

—that he could sympathize in a way. He blew the thin fog of feeling out of his mind. That kind of sympathy is the end of the professional attitude; you become a patient yourself. "Well," he said almost sharply, "you went to the window."

"Yes," Innes hurried on. "I opened it; I Am ran in, trotted to the fire, waited for me to sit down. I sat down; own, I didn't take up my book; own, I hadn't been reading it before he knocked. But this time he didn't have any queer second thoughts. I began to think the act was over. He was back on the old rails. For, sure enough, he chose his spot on the hearth—there, just where your feet are—and started on his grooming. It was all so reassuring. After all, it's one of the most reassuring sights there is: that sane, methodical, pleasant body-conscious self-centeredness. Women brushing their hair, they're always thinking of some man and what he'll say about it. But a cat's pleasure is sanely animal. I watched a few minutes, watched until, all clear and clean, he stretched out one paw and then the other one, found everything at ease, curled up, and went to sleep. It was such a persuasively pantomime sermon on the virtue of relaxation; he was practicing so well what he preached and demonstrated that it had me convinced. I smiled at myself." Innes smiled wanly at the memory of his last relief, as the sun itself, already overwhelmed by storm clouds, throws up against them a last pallid shaft of light.

"I picked up my book and found my place. It was a good novel of detective adventure. I was soon well settled: my body snug in this chair, my mind ranging off with the story teller or now and then following its own speculations. I don't know how long I read. I suppose I must have stirred, crossed my legs or something, and that may have done it; set it off. Anyhow, I looked up over the edge of my book to the hearth. There was the cat on it. But he was no longer curled up asleep. He was awake and, as I've said, some move of mine may have done it. Anyhow, he was looking up at me."

He stopped. Hamilton cut in. "Yes, that's common in cats. I myself have often noticed it. You disturb them; they look up at you and then forget, but also forget to turn their heads. They've never been taught it's rude to stare. After all," he chuckled rather deliberately, "cats wouldn't have been told they could look at kings unless they'd first shown a taste for this bland, contemptuous interest in human self-consciousness."

Innes wasn't listening. He was getting ready to make an avowal, dreadful to himself, ridiculous to his companion. At last he collected the words, "I looked at I Am; he at me—a sort of strange staring match, I thought for a little. And then I noticed something else. You know how all cats' eyes flash when at night a car's headlights catch them, say, when they're crossing a road. You'd know also that the pale blue eyes of the Siamese are really nearly pigmentless; they are almost albinos." Hamilton grunted assent. "Well, then, perhaps you have noticed another thing. If you're sitting like this, with your back to a strong light, such as this reading lamp with its reflector, and the focused light, of course, is thrown straight into the cat's eyes, then, not only are its slit-pupils nearly closed and all the eye nearly covered by the iris, but all the color goes from the eye—it appears like a pink mirror."

"Of course," said the Doctor, "you're looking right into the eye itself."

"Well, all I know is that then it gives the effect . . ." he went over the sentence again, "it gives the effect of looking into a small, lit room, lit with a warm firelight, cosy, quiet, but waiting for someone to come in and occupy it." He closed his sentence with an ancient quotation: " 'empty, swept, and garnished.' "I went on looking into those small binocular, stereoscopic mirrors. I suppose the cat and I were both in a kind of reciprocal trance. Anyhow, gradually I began to think that I was actually looking into a mirror and that in that mirror was reflected this room. The cat's eyes would then be showing me this room. You see," he went on more slowly, "I would be seeing this room, seeing behind me all of the other wall right along to the window."

Innes pointed over his shoulder with his left hand but kept his eyes on the hearth. "I saw it all perfectly clearly, like a view down the wrong end of a telescope. It was in minute but sharpest-cut detail. I scanned every bit of it with the lazy curiosity with which one looks into a camera obscura. Things reduced to model size are somehow always intriguing. I worked my attention along, or rather my eye shifted out to the very edge of the picture, right out to where that window," again he didn't turn around but pointed with a hooked-back finger in the direction, "terminated my view. I went to it and glanced at the curtain on the left. You see it is a heavy thick curtain and, as now, it was drawn back, since I had not replaced it when I had let in the cat. And then," Innes' voice had become a whisper and Hamilton had to lean over to catch the words, "I saw the room was—

not—not quite as it had been when I had last looked at it. Something else had—been added. By the thick folds of the curtain—I had blinked my own eyes twice to see that they were not cheating me, I looked carefully twice into the mirror-eyes before I could be sure. But then I was as sure as that you're in that chair—" his voice rose to an unpleasantly shrill dismay. "There in the corner by the curtain, watching me, was something, someone, standing ready, ready . . ."

He swung round. The panic infection of his voice was too strong for the doctor. He, too, could not keep his head from swiveling over his shoulder. He gasped with relief, and then with disgust at himself. The room was healthily empty as a meadow. He flung a glance at Innes, who with incredulous relief was also gazing at the curtain.

Hamilton sprang up, strode across the room, and shook the heavy velvet—"The commonest form of hallucination," he exclaimed. "Why, Walter Scott, that sane old tale-teller, says he was almost frightened out of his life by seeing, in the dusk, his dressing gown look like a dead friend."

"But," Innes muttered, "but it wasn't in the room itself, at least not yet, not then, that I saw it. It was in that creature's eyes."

For a moment Dr. Hamilton stood by the window. He'd probably do best to go across to Innes and give him a good shaking. Hysterics are now, once again, being slapped into remembering that they are sane; he recalled reading that only a week ago, in his favorite medical journal. Maybe it's not much use to the hysteric, but what a blessed relief to the doctor. Could he really slap an old, respectable, not well-liked friend? He hesitated. What would have happened if he had acted on the notion, who knows. But in those four or five seconds in which he delayed and Innes waited, the next thing happened.

The room was empty and silent, but suddenly they were both arrested. "Bump, Bump." Innes had heard it; he was half out of his chair. Yes, there could be no doubt. Hamilton glanced at his watch—nine-thirty, precisely. It was not a considered reaction, but all he could say, was, "Well, that isn't a tap; it's a kind of bump."

Innes was already passing him on his way to the window. "On time," was all he said. Hamilton had only to wheel round and they were both abreast of the dark window. They looked down to the lowest pane at floor level. In the light thrown out past them by the lit room behind, they could see a faint object.

"It's I Am," said Innes. Hamilton couldn't clearly discern that it was a cat at all. If it was, it must be muffled in some way. What was obvious was that Innes was going into complete panic. There'd be an awful scene if he didn't somehow stop the whole fantasy. He gripped the bolt lever and threw open the window. Over the threshold at their feet hopped a smoke-gray cat. Of course it had been hard to see it outside, for its face was nearly hidden in black feathers. In its jaws was a fairly large bird, and the wretched creature was still alive.

With a natural reaction Hamilton struck the cat, dealing it a stinging slap on the back of the head. It sprung back, dropping its prey, and bounded out into the garden. The heap of blood-stained feathers lay on the floor a moment. Then the twisted body began to try and pull itself together.

They could see that the head and neck were crushed down under the body. It was trying to get them free. Both Innes and Hamilton drew back, one shrinking to touch the mangled body, the other wondering whether he had not better step on it quickly and so break its neck. The body drew itself up; the neck and head nearly emerged. At that moment both of them heard, rising from the wreckage, a small, hoarse, ghost-of-a-voice. "Are you deaf then?" it questioned.

The feathers flopped. Hamilton, with thumb and finger, lifted the limp dead body of the blackbird. Over at the fire he cleared a place in the blazing logs, dropped the carrion in, and flung after it three or four handfuls of kindling. The fire shot up with a crackle and filled the whole hearth. Then he turned to Innes. He was still looking at the small blood stain and some smeared down-feathers that clung to the carpet. "Come and sit down," he said. "Cats are cruel little beasts, but they can't help it. In the blood; merely reflex, instinct."

He owned to himself that that dirty little incident, coming where and when it did, couldn't have been more inapposite —or should he say apposite? Such questions were grotesque. Innes was having bad luck, and that was all. Here, for the first time, was a real coincidence, barging in, to fling a spot of trouble on a nervous case which had gone further than he'd first fancied and further than—in another sense of that odd word—he now quite fancied. He went toward Innes but stopped at the bookcase.

Innes swung past him and, keeping his eyes on the curtain, drew back to the chairs. But he spoke to Hamilton: "I don't blame the cat—any more than I blame the bird."

Then with a sudden blaze of terror exploding into rage: "Don't you see, you hell-fool Hamilton. Don't you see? They were simply pawns, messengers. Don't you see? I've been stalked: stalked so assuredly, so cleverly that the stalker actually gives warnings that he's on my track. Dares me to shake him off. See, he's ready to start as soon as I'll call him up. Yes, he knew I'd called him. I'd wanted to kill her, my wife. Night after night, I've come in here to get away from her. Her voice, saying "Are you deaf"—God how I've longed to silence it. I've sat here night after night praying for a safe, sure way, a way that everyone would think natural. I know there's lots of ways. I've sat in that chair saying to myself, that if I just sit quiet and still it will steal into my mind, the perfect traceless way—just as a forgotten word comes in, while you wait, looking, as it were, in the other direction. Then the next signal, *The Frontier Is Crossed,* he's on his way. The third—then I saw he had me—I was to be the victim, not she—I'm the poor stupid fish. He gave his timetable then, from the first reply to my call till his arrival. Oh, he's a fine timekeeper. He runs on schedule. The next night he shows me he's at my shoulder, at my back, standing over me, ready to strike. Tonight, with perfect irony, in your presence—you whom I've asked to save me, you a starched shirt stuffed with stupid self-assurance—tonight he asks me, 'Am I deaf?' No, I'm not deaf; I'm not blind now. The poor fish sees and hears as the spear gets it!"

Innes's eyes were now watching something at the curtain with such intensity that Hamilton could not but believe that there was a "presence" between him and the wretched maniac. It was all the more horribly convincing as he saw

Innes's eyes drawing in their focus, and, a moment after, Innes's body creeping back, as though giving way before someone approaching him. But, of course, he couldn't give way.

"Take care!" shouted Hamilton. But Innes, dreading something else far more, had stumbled back into the leaping fire.

Hamilton snatched him out. "Shock," he said, trying to pull himself together, when it was clear there was no use trying any longer to pull the patient round. "Of course, I knew that he'd got to hate her like hell. But naturally he hadn't the nerve to pull off a murder—or even a suicide. But it's the fatal shock all right. And," he paused in his quick muttering to himself, "were all those—happenings coincidences? Better call the police. Thank heaven, they're even more spirit-proof than we doctors. Still, it's one more queer story for a posthumous case-book."

THE ROUSING OF MR. BRADEGAR

MR. BRADEGAR WAS not alarmed. That would have been an exaggeration, and a disparaging exaggeration—which is, in itself, so unusual as to awaken doubt. But Mr. Bradegar had been waked in an unusual way, in a way which—he would have been quite happy to allow it, had there been anyone to make happy by the allowance—might well have been alarming to a more highly strung nature. Indeed, the trouble about this sudden summons back from dreams to reality was that Mr. Bradegar was quite at a loss to know what it was that had summoned him. It was not "rosy-fingered dawn." A glance hadn't shown much—indeed, had shown so little that it seemed clear that dawn wasn't in the offing and would not be for a long while; otherwise you ought to see where "the casement grows a glimmering square." No—if he had his bearings right—it is hard to be sure when you are waked too quickly—but to the best of his knowledge, the window was where he was looking, and there was no suspicion of a glimmering square about it. Well, ears might be better than eyes. With the fingers of his upper hand, which, with its under fellow, had been folded near his face in the attitude of fetal humility, which we resume when he would rest, Mr. Bradegar got ready to push back the edge of the sheet, under which he lay up to the ears—then paused.

What was that? A rustle? No, it was only the small sound made as his too-vigilant ear moved on its own, obeying an impulse almost as ancient as his sleeping pose, trying to cock itself, but only succeeding now in producing a small sound—the sound of its own movement against the sheet edge—instead of detecting an external disturbance. He must have his ears clear if his eyes wouldn't work. There, now he was unlapped. It was his good ear, too; so he must be lying on his left side! so, again, he must be right about the window and, further, about the time, within limits. It was his good ear, because he could hear the discrete pulse of the mantel clock. Yes, he was now quite awake and had himself well arranged in relation to his whereabouts. He noticed, too, that his heart was beating more slowly. He reflected on this. "I must have had a start in my sleep. Perhaps it was only a dream."

He worked the back of his neck a little deeper into the pillow until he was quite comfortable, gave up staring into the dark, but still left his "weather ear" uncovered. Half over on his back, he could keep a casual watch until sleep relieved him. It evidently was closer at hand than he thought, for in no perceptible length of time he found himself of the opinion that he was out in the street, just about to cross, when a small dog ran in front of him, turned its head, and barked sharply, "Wake up!" Mr. Bradegar obeyed instantly and, as instantly, he was aware that the same whatever-it-was that had first startled him to wakefulness must have done it again. His ear was still uncovered; the window still as noncommittal; only the mantel clock, after a soft preliminary whirring, began to strike—if strike is not too emphatic a word for its perfect night-nurse manner. But it hadn't much to say: "One, Two."

Mr. Bradegar also noticed again that his heart had evidently caught on to this thing even before it had waked him. It was slackening down from a more rapid pace. "Dormio, sed cor . . ." he quoted to himself.

Two A.M. The heart should now be at its slowest. Poor old thing, having to put in some overbeats, when it should be on its half time. Mr. Bradegar was sensibly concerned—not alarmed—about his heart. "Guest and companion of my clay," he quoted again; a little more sadly and secularly this time; for sixty years beating away to get him enough energy—to be born, to fight at school, row himself blind at college, pull himself, for a dozen seasons, to the top of two score Alpine "first-class" peaks, and leap down the throats of "the opposing attorney" and his witnesses, day after day, for half a lifetime. It was a reputable record for a soft piece of sinew which has to be as precise as the best clockwork and as ready as a rattler. He must give it a chance. That is what Wilkinshaw, the big heart man, had said. "Give it a chance—" and give me a hundred dollars for asking you to do what you intend! Easy job, these big doctors; easier than ours in the courts. I'd never have been able to pay to ask him to disapprove of the pace I've had to live at if I hadn't worked harder than he ever had to work. "Give it a chance!" I never could let my heart or anyone else have a chance till I was over fifty. Heart and head, lungs and liver, kidneys and skin, all had to stand the racket, or give if they couldn't.

That was why he was alone. Mabel wouldn't stand for it, nor the two girls. They sided with their mother. Girls usually don't. One of them nearly always likes her father. But both went with Mabel. "Mental cruelty!" If all day you've been getting their living, and they wanted a lot, by watching like a pike to see if the other fellow couldn't be snapped up, you couldn't turn off the trick when you came home. You'd got into the way of striking as quickly, as surely, as automatically as a sidewinder. Well, they wouldn't stand for it. So here he was now with his heart to watch, and nothing else. He'd done well and, he'd hoped, as soon as he was through with getting on, he'd get liked. He'd do the things—he'd have time—that get you liked: the big, generous things with which the big, easy, famous men convince everyone, everyone who now wants to forget that they were ever small, keen, mean. They're formidable still, of course, but in such a grand way. They just go on getting their way, but with no more than an inflection of the voice—they don't have so much as to raise a finger any longer. The old proverbial success of success. But— "Where are the monuments of those who were drowned?" "Nothing succeeds like succession: nothing succeeds like surcease." The phrase "declined" itself, as one used to say of verbs in school grammar lessons. . . . He was trying to memorize the whole conjugation. There was only a little time. The clock above the desks showed that the preparation hour was nearly over. He had learned all the other irregular verbs but this silly one: "Success, succession, surcease"—How did the rest of it go? "Success, succession, surcease, decease, death, cremation"—that was it—not a very irregular verb, after all: you could tell each declension from the one before pretty well. He'd be able to remember it when called out to say it in front of the class. He looked up at the clock again. It was just going to strike the hour but, instead, it remarked in a sharper tone of voice, "Wake up!"

Mr. Bradegar once more sprang to attention to find as before that he was horizontal, sheet-swathed, pillow-sunk—and had once more missed the tide. He *had* been called, but by the time he'd hurried up to the doors of his body, the summoner, like a "ring-and-run" street urchin, had made off. But had it? Mr. Bradegar's mood, which had nearly risen to the vigorous daylight state of irritated disappointment, suddenly sank, sank to apprehension. Perhaps he wasn't going to be disappointed this time? Perhaps, this time, the ringer hadn't run?

He was now fully awake and realized how keenly sorry he was that he wasn't going to be disappointed. "This is the third time I've been roused," he remarked to himself. There was a gentle whirring, and, as if in answer to his half-question, the clock announced that it was Three. But, whether it was because he was more awake this time, the tone of voice in which his timepiece made this, its third, summons to a new day, struck Mr. Bradegar as being a trifle more peremptory, less deferential than the discreet summons of an hour ago. Then it had almost seemed to say by its tone, "Excuse me, Sir, but should you be wishing to know the precise hour, I beg to inform you that it is just two A.M." Now its stroke rather suggested, "Take it or leave it," with perhaps even a hint of, "But if you do slip off again I'm not responsible if you never wake up in time."

But what was Mr. Bradegar meant to do? He was roused, but for what? The only thing was to set oneself to listen. Putting on the light wouldn't throw any on what might be present but which always seemed just to have done what it was up to and escaped into the past. "If I did put on the light," he reflected, "I'd only have the unpleasant feeling that whatever it is that's nibbling at me had been looking right at me the moment before I pressed the switch." That thought was so unpleasantly convincing that Mr. Bradegar, who had been vainly peering over the sheet's fold into the dark, involuntarily shut his eyes—only for a moment, he felt sure. But the clock had another opinion. Mr. Bradegar was all ears as, having started striking, as if worked up to a kind of angry protest, the clock went on making its points like a lawyer pressing a conviction: "One, Two, Three, Four." "What?" thought Mr. Bradegar. "Five, Six." Six! And there was no doubt that the clock's tone was as harshly startling as the information it imparted.

Mr. Bradegar's attention flooded from ears to eyes. He opened them, found the sheet was over them, pushed it aside with an impatiently anxious finger—and, in a flash, realized what had happened. His whole body signaled it. Every sense, with a sort of cannonading broadside, thundered the fact. He blinked his eyes—yes, the room was light, but he could see only faintly, blurredly. He moved his legs, yes, with difficulty. He knew at once: he was not the sort of fool that fools himself. He knew how to diagnose that curious sense of constriction, that feeling as though one were walking along the foot of the bed, that imaginary sensation. Of course, it was the typical projection phenomenon, the massive sensation-pattern similar to the acute nerve response which the leg-amputation patient feels when he says his toes are being pinched.

Mr. Bradegar again stretched a little, to be quite sure. Yes, there wasn't a shadow of doubt—that illusion of being restricted, of touching the foot of the bed, could mean only one thing. He knew he couldn't actually be doing so, because, as it happened, he'd had that bed built to make impossible precisely that horizontal nocturnal ambulation. As a boy he'd hated a too-short bed in which he'd been made to go on sleeping when he'd outgrown it—really a child's cot—and he'd made a promise to himself, which he'd kept, that when he grew up he'd have a footless bed and one in which, stretch as you would, you just couldn't touch the end. Mabel had laughed at him and, later, had been annoyed. He'd grown to be a tall man. She'd said a seven-foot bed was nonsense—looked positively unbalanced. He'd replied that a bed was balanced if it stood steady on its four feet and, anyhow, it wasn't for looks but for closing your eyes in. Of course, she'd replied that, at least as long as they were up and about, she didn't see why her mouth should be shut by his snapping. It was one of those useless, fruitless, but fecund quarrels. They'd found by then that they could quarrel over anything, by the time he was making enough money for her always to be wanting more, and he without any time but to make it.

He felt with his foot once more. Not a doubt of it. Well, he'd like to see Mabel's face when she heard the news—remorse for a moment, then relief—until his lawyer, whom she'd ring up quick enough, gave her the will in brief.

Thinking of Mabel's face reminded him to repeat the visual check-up. He opened his eyes again, which had closed as he felt about with his feet under the bedclothes. True enough, eyes answered to toes, repeating the first message that they'd given him at the clock's summons. His eyes confirmed the numbed constricted feeling of his legs, interpreting the general condition in their particular terms. He was seeing as blurredly as he felt numbly. He'd face the music: those starts in the night, he knew now exactly what they were. One, two, three, the little lesions had taken place. He'd had a serial stroke: he was quite extensively paralyzed.

He pulled himself together inwardly, as outwardly he must leave himself sprawled—"As the tree falls, so shall it lie." He was alone in the house (he began his summary of his situation), not in pain—well, that was a reasonable expectation. But, more, he felt wonderfully light and fresh. Indeed, if he hadn't known beyond a doubt that he was extensively paralyzed and perhaps on the verge of death, he would actually—funny thought (he began actually to chuckle), he would have thought he was wonderfully well—indeed, years younger than when he had crawled under the sheets to begin the night.

He wished a moment that he'd troubled to ask his other friends who'd had strokes whether they'd felt this lightness, freshness, this absurd sense of being free and careless. Perhaps they had all felt it. He'd often heard doctors say that many of the insane are happier than when they had their wits. Consumptives, too, they're peculiarly optimistic just before their final hemorrhage. So it would be that when your brain is wrecked you have illusions of being young, a sort of mental face lifting—he chuckled again, and the thought floated out of his mind. He felt so careless and so easy that it wasn't worth thinking about anything very long. That was perhaps the funniest part about it all—to be so completely at one's ease, to feel so well in one's body that one didn't care about anything else, when, as a matter of fact, everything, mind, body, and estate were gone.

Yes, everything: for he now realized that not only was he helplessly paralyzed and his sight blurred but his mind was rapidly going. That was it—the brain hemorrhage must be spreading rapidly. He couldn't think now of what he'd last been thinking, only a moment ago! What was that thing he meant to ask old sick men about? Something to do with what they felt when they were ill. Oh, well, it didn't matter. What would he be wanting to do, bothering old wrecks about what they felt or didn't feel! His mind was so light and gay that he couldn't keep it more than a moment on anything. And that, too, he found rather fun. Still, as things ran through his mind, it was jolly just to run after them, as it were. To keep track of the carnival, he began to talk aloud to himself as a sort of comment on his thoughts. Evidently his speech was left, or at least it seemed so.

But, before he'd time to check up on that, his voice was joined by another, or rather was collided into by it. "Don't keep on murmuring to yourself like that," it said.

He stopped and listened. Another sound broke on his ear. It was a sort of breathless howl. A breathless howl? Why, of course, that was a *yawn!* Someone was in the room and was waking up. Mr. Bradegar raised his head—so that, too, wasn't paralyzed. And that movement discovered something else for him—his eyes hadn't suddenly failed; fact was, they were as fresh as his mind. He laughed. He'd fancied he was going blind because his nose almost had been touching the raised wooden sidepiece of the bed head—that silly boy's bed in which he was still made to sleep though he was far too big for it and could never stretch his legs. He flung them over the edge. What was that dream about his not being able to move? The sort of nightmare one would get in a suffocating little bunk like this. But he'd dreamed a lot more than that. If he could catch the whole spiel before it slipped away, he'd remember all sorts of odd things. Gosh! it was a dream as long as *David Copperfield;* longer, by gum—all about all sorts of things: being a success and arguing people down, far better than at the school debating club, and meeting a wonderful girl.

But, somehow, she didn't, he recollected faintly, turn out to be so wonderful after all. And other girls, small girls, small girls that he'd liked because they were small. But that was getting out of one's depth. How could one like little girls! He couldn't think up much more incident—only a general impression remained that he'd had a crackerjack dream—not so nice in its way, but wonderful just because it had seemed so confounded real, as real as one's own life, as real as oneself in this little old sleeping room and Uncle Andy still snoozing in the big bed by the window.

Uncle Andy yawned again, snuffled, and remarked, "You been talking in your dreams jest like one of them thar Edison sound boxes I've jest been hearing of. You've gotten indigestion—eating all that punkin pie las' night."

"It's this silly little bed. It gives me cramps. I was somehow fixed so I got dreaming I couldn't ever move again."

"Indigestion; overdistended stummuck. You get a move on."

"Well, I feel fine this morning."

"Then get up and don't sit there yarning at me and complaining of your good bed that's held you well enough these twelve years."

Uncle Andy was always a little sore in the mornings, Nick Bradegar remembered. Still, as he got out to fetch his towel and to go into the yard to splash under the pump, he felt, suddenly, that he must stop and ask a question. Why? It was the sort to make Uncle Andy sore. Still, something in the back of his mind made him feel it worth the risk.

"Uncle, what's it like really to be grown up, to be as old as you are?"

Over the crumpled sheet of the big bed a rheumy eye regarded him. He thought he was going to be bawled out. But no voice came. Only the old, tired, inflamed eye kept on looking at him—first, fiercely, next, defiantly, then, pathetically—that was worst. Or was it? For suddenly it didn't seem Uncle Andy's eye any longer. It seemed somehow a picture of some sort, a kind of mirror, or as though you were looking down the wrong end of a telescope. Ever so small and distant, but quite clear, he saw an old man lying with fixed, open eyes on a long bed. The light was still faint, as though the window had a curtain over it. The old man lay stiffly still, all save the lid of his eye, which seemed to flicker a bit as he lay on his side looking toward Nick. He was awful like Uncle Andy, and yet, somehow, he wasn't Uncle. The bed, too, looked far richer, just as the man in it looked even more tired than Andy.

The old, harsh clock began to strike, but it seemed more soft than usual. Still, it was enough to rouse Uncle. "You get along, you young lazy scamp. There's the half-hour gone and you still not even washed. You leave me alone with all your darn questions. You'll know soon enough what it is to be old—the heck you will! And, I'll lay it, you'll not have made the hand at living I've made when time comes to take a stretch, as I've a right to take. Get along and don't disturb me till you've the coffee ready and the bacon cooked!"

He nipped out of the room. If you didn't clear quickly when Uncle blew like that, you'd have his boots flying at your head a moment after, and, though old and lying down, Uncle had scored more hits than misses with those old hobnails of his, which were always close at hand when off his feet.

Under the yard pump the cold water on the top of his head made his brain tingle. Like rockets, thoughts shot through his mind. He wouldn't be a failure, like Uncle, or just conk out, the way he'd heard his parents had. He'd get through and make good. Why, he could always win in discussions at school, already. He was always twice as quick at answering back or thinking up a wisecrack. Yes, and some of those big hulks and lubbers who could kick him over a fence, they were afraid of his tongue, he knew—the way things he said would stick to the person he said 'em about. He saw himself getting on. What did one do? Law, of course. As he rubbed his red, thin body with the coarse towel, he saw himself on his feet in court, winning big law cases, first here and there and then right and left; then marrying, of course, an admiring wife and having a large family that'd look up to him, because he was clever, rich, powerful.

He went in and started cooking the breakfast in the old squalid kitchen. But he hardly smelled the bacon and coffee, so strong was the daydream on him. Only the sound of Uncle's boots on the stairs, now, fortunately, on his old lame feet and not in his still flexible hands, roused him.

"Now, go and make the beds, you lazy fellow. I know you! If you have your breakfast first, then you never have time. You've got to go off to that darned school! Where they only teach you what you were born doing and do in your sleep and'll be doing when you die in the poorhouse—talk, talk, talk. Get along with you!"

Nick Bradegar cut out of the kitchen and ran up the stairs into the frowzy bedroom. On the big bed he swung the old frayed stale sheets, worn blankets, and tattered coverlet into some sort of uneasy order. When he came to his cot, however, he paused, looking with a sort of helpless anger at the queer little cramped bed.

"Well, all I know," he remarked to himself with vicious resolution, "if ever I make even a hundred bucks, I'll have a decent bed. First thing I'll have, I promise myself that. You spend nearly half your life on that one thing. Gum, if I could have a fine decent bed, I don't think I'd mind anything else much. You'd always be able to stretch yourself in that to your heart's content. And in a fine bed you can have fine dreams. That nightmare last night—what was it? It's all gone, but the taste. I know the cause, though—that blasted little bed!"

"Here, you come down! What ye doing all this while?" holloed Uucle Andy from below. "And wash up 'fore you go to that darned school!"

Printed in Great Britain
by Amazon